HOW TO ROPE A ROUGH COWBOY

SILVER SPRINGS RANCH: BOOK 3

ANYA SUMMERS

Published by S & G Books LLC
P.O. Box 3353
Ballwin, Missouri 63022
USA

How To Rope A Rough Cowboy
Anya Summers

This is a work of fiction. Names, places, businesses, characters, and incidents
are either the product of the author's imagination or are used in a fictitious
manner. Any resemblance to actual persons living or dead, actual events or
locales is purely coincidental.

Photos By Period Images

Print ISBN 979-8-7303427-1-2

Ebook ISBN 978-1-7356398-7-1

ABOUT THE BOOK

Maverick Greyson is barely housebroken. Having been raised on ranches, he spends the bulk of his days on the back of his horse, and can't imagine a finer way to occupy his time – except maybe a night with a willing female. He loves women. Enjoys their company mightily. Relishes the available bounty of tourists and townsfolk alike, and rarely enjoys the same woman twice.

But the ranch's newest guest, Bianca Peabody, makes him want to swear off the species entirely. The doe-eyed beauty, with her highfalutin' attitude, makes his blood boil.

And yet the sorrow he glimpses in her one night changes everything. Now his soul hungers to have her in his arms. He burns for her love. Heaven help him, her surrender may be everything he has always needed.

For the first time in his life, Maverick is looking toward the future, and building one with the only woman he has ever wanted to claim. But she is keeping secrets...

Secrets capable of destroying him – and any future they might have.

1

---

*B*ugger it.

Bianca contemplated for the hundredth time tonight whether she had finally lost her mind as she boarded the overnight flight from Heathrow to Dulles, and took her seat in first class. Fleeing seemed to be her only option. She could practically hear her mum saying she was being overly dramatic and needed to fall in line. That Peabodys never backed down from their responsibilities to uphold family traditions.

Regardless of whether Bianca thought they were archaic and should have been buried a hundred years ago.

She snapped her seatbelt into place, trying not to fidget in her beige khaki trousers and ivory blouse while the rest of the passengers boarded, battling back fear that somehow, she would be prevented from escaping. That her mother would discover the hastily scrawled note she had left on the dining table in her flat before the plane left the airport, use her multitude of high-ranking connections, and have a member of the defense ministry keep the flight from departing, whereupon Bianca would then be escorted off to face condemnation, and a life sentence.

But she had to get away for some dearly needed space, and hopefully achieve a smattering of clarity. She was exhausted from trying to please everyone, from pretending to be someone she was not, and trying to live as her mother expected her to instead of doing what *she* wanted with her life.

Those expectations extended to the places she went, where she lived, the people she interacted with and called her friends, and even whom she was supposed to marry. Out of them all, it was that last bit that was the hardest to swallow.

"Good evening folks, this is Captain Barrow. I'm here with my co-pilot, Watts. If everyone could please take their seats, that way, we can depart on time. We'll be backing away from the gate in just a few moments. We have one stop in Dublin, then we'll be continuing our flight on to Washington D.C. Travel time for this flight is thirteen hours and fifty-six minutes. Weather over the Atlantic should be smooth sailing. Sit back, relax, and welcome aboard. Cabin crew, prepare the cabin for take-off, please."

Time slowed to a crawl. When the flight attendant sealed the plane door shut, Bianca gripped the armrests of her seat, mainly to keep herself from flinging off the seatbelt and rushing the door like a mad woman to exit the plane.

What stopped her cold and kept her in her seat?

The knowledge that, if she left the plane, she would die.

Not in the physical sense, perhaps, but on a soul deep level. Today, as she had stood in her white gown with her mother and friends all excitedly chatting, the walls had started caving in, strangling her as all the air was sucked from the room. It took every ounce of strength inside her not to hyperventilate and pass out.

She didn't love Peter.

Not as anything more than a lifelong friend. They had never dated each other, not in the traditional sense of the word. They had never had sex. The most intimate the two of them had ever been had been to give each other brief kisses. And the only sensation that bubbled to the surface when they kissed: it was as if Bianca was kissing her brother —if she had one, and Peter was the closest thing to it. They had grown up together. They cared for one another. There was no doubt in her mind about that. They enjoyed each other's company.

But there was absolutely no passion or desire. She wasn't in love with him. Nor was he in love with her. They had family obligation and tradition hanging over their heads like the Grim Reaper's scythe.

And then, of course, they had the same boorish, social climbing, entitled peer circle, combined with family expectations to marry well.

Bianca had allowed her parents—her mother, mostly—to browbeat her into the formal engagement. Her concession had solidified the arrangement their parents had agreed upon when she was thirteen and Peter sixteen.

At twenty-eight, Bianca had known the impending marriage was on the horizon, barreling toward her like an avalanche. Their parents had never hidden the deal they had made for them.

Which was why, six months ago when her mum had compelled her to make it official, like a bleeding coward, Bianca hadn't fought her. Her mother always ended up bullying Bianca until she caved and got her way in everything, anyway. There was no point in kicking up a stink.

Most days, Bianca questioned whose life it really was to begin with—hers, or her mother's. After conceding to her mother's pressure, she had handed over all the control to her mum, allowing her to make the arrangements for everything for the wedding ceremony, from her dress, to who her bridesmaids would be, to the decorations, the catering... and on and on. Because Bianca didn't care about the wedding. She didn't want it. She never had.

She didn't have the energy necessary to invest in it herself.

But then a strange thing had happened today as she stood decked out in the wedding gown for one of the final dress fittings, with six weeks to go until the nuptials. The walls had closed in around her and she had been seized with mind-numbing panic. It had taken all Bianca's strength not to run out of the dressmaker's shop, with her only thought being escaping the coming doom.

Her entire existence was rubbish. A hell she had no hope of vacating.

While her mother and bridesmaids had all chatted excitedly, Bianca had stood stock still, a fake smile frozen in place, fighting increasing alarm, only to have a plan form, an escape hatch so that she could finally breathe again.

Not long after the dressmaker finished with her, she exited the festivities, claiming she felt unwell. The panic had made her hands and forehead clammy, which convinced her mother she needed a lie down.

The moment she got back into her flat, Bianca had booked the last-minute flight to the United States, and contacted her broker to have funds transferred into an account she had set up a few years back that her mother had no idea existed. And then, like a mad woman, she had packed her bags in a flurry of activity. She penned a letter to her parents and Peter, saying that she needed time away before the big day, and would return a few days before the ceremony, and left the letter on the dining room table where her mother would find it.

When Bianca didn't answer her calls, her mum would barge in with her key to discover what could possibly be keeping her from answering the phone. She gave herself a day—maybe two—before her mother stopped by.

Which was why, as soon as her things were packed, Bianca had called for a cab and had it ferry her to Heathrow. If she had stayed in her flat and waited, she would have wimped out. Once her bags were checked and she was past security, she was stuck. It was far too ingrained in her not to make anything resembling a fuss, and leaving the gate to request her luggage back was a commotion that would cause waves. She had dinner—what little she could eat given the jumbled mess of her nervous stomach—and watched planes take off as she waited for her flight.

The time away would provide her the opportunity to get still without her mother's constant bullying, and decide if she could really go through with the marriage. Because when she envisioned the arc of her life, if she continued down this path with the way things stood, there were parts of her that would die.

And her greatest fear would be realized. Deep down, Bianca knew marrying Peter would turn her into her mother: bitter, and obsessed with her status in society.

It was why she had rebelled at various intervals throughout her life, even though it had been years since she had drummed up the courage to deviate from her mother's plans for her.

Bianca didn't fit in with her peers. She never had. They looked down their upturned noses at her. It didn't help that interactions with them made her nervous and she always managed to say the wrong thing. Truth be told, she thought the lot of them were insipid, shallow individuals all trying to clobber each other for the right to lord their status over one another.

Running away for some much needed time to ponder her situation, to a place her mother would never suspect she would visit, was beyond necessary. Unfortunately, the United States capital was still too close to her mother's reach. Bianca had learned that the hard way when she'd studied art in Rome for two years. After her flight landed at Dulles in the morning, she would have breakfast in Washington before boarding a second flight to the middle of the country, and then driving for two hours into the wilds of the American west.

The plane taxied down the runway and made its initial ascent. When they were finally airborne, Bianca slid the sleep mask down over her eyes, praying that the half of a Xanax pill she had taken before boarding would settle her anxiety down, and maybe even knock her out for the duration of the flight.

As the aircraft reached cruising altitude, her internal panic waned and faded. She could no longer feel the Reaper's scythe being held against her windpipe. Calmness descended over her, and she drifted off to sleep.

———

ON HIS WAY home that evening, Maverick tapped his fingers on the steering wheel of his black truck. The participants of the last two trail rides should be back at the stables soon. He trusted Taylor and Wyatt to handle the horses currently out upon their return, and ensure they were groomed and fed. The rest of the stock had already been fed, and were bedded down for the night.

Jeremiah was on overnight duty, and staying in the stables. With the multitude of horses in the Silver Springs Ranch stock, they liked to have a wrangler present at night in case of emergency. They had a bunk room for the wrangler to get some shut eye. But the safety measure had worked time and time again. It was why they continued putting a man on duty on a weekly rotation.

Mav veered off the main ranch drive. He had a cabin about a mile away from the main hub with stables, the hotel, and guest cabins. It was secluded, surrounded by pines, and one of the closest places to Cabin X—which was off limits to guests. As Doms, he and his buddies took willing submissives there when they wanted to scene. They tended to reserve the cabin when needed, and then had a group night once a month, for those who preferred exhibitionism and voyeurism.

It was Saturday evening, and a bunch of the guys who were off the clock were heading to the Bucking Bronco in town. It was the local watering hole, where they tended to pick up locals and tourists alike. It was where Cabin X sub favorite Maribella worked as a waitress.

But Mav wasn't up for crowds tonight. Nor had he been in the mood for them much lately—mainly because he was saving every penny he could to build his house. He figured he would head home, grill up a steak, pop open a beer, and watch baseball on the flatscreen. While not an exciting thrill ride like tying a woman to his bed and fucking her blind, it worked for him.

A few months back, he had bought thirty-six acres of Rocky Mountain wilderness from Colt Anderson before his buddy had headed off with the little scientist, Avery, to travel the world. The property Mav had purchased ran adjacent to Silver Springs Ranch, was just the prettiest spot, and it all belonged to him—every blade of grass, every rock and tree, even the small brook that cut through the acreage, was his.

At his current salary, Mav figured it would take him another eighteen months of saving to have the necessary funds to build his house and barn. But he would do it, just as he had worked and saved the last half a dozen years to own his own property so that one day he would live in his own house instead of a place that was afforded him as part of his salary.

It meant that, when it came to partners of the nubile female variety, his current dance card had been fairly empty. Luckily for him, there were enough single tourists who blew through the ranch on vacation that he knew he could find enough to keep him sated over the upcoming peak summer months.

As he drove past a group of guest cabins, a smile lit his face at spotting a possible new quarry to entice into his bed.

Bingo!

He ogled the blonde beauty without her knowledge. Her deep golden tresses were drawn back in a sedate pony-tail that hung down her slim back. His gaze drifted south as he slowed his truck. A punch of lust spread through him. Without a doubt, the woman had one of the most spectac-ular asses he'd beheld in a week of Sundays. Her tan slacks molded to her shapely butt and slender legs. She was bent over, fishing suitcases out of a rental car trunk, and it looked like she was having a rather difficult time lifting them.

As an employee of Silver Springs Ranch, it was his responsibility to stop and assist a guest in dire need. And if her front was as attractive as the back end, Mav figured he might have found a new conquest he could charm into letting him tie her to his bed so they could spend the night screwing one another's brains out.

Mav parked his truck along the curb. His window was rolled down due to the nice, balmy weather of the May day, which meant he heard her dulcet, cultured voice perfectly when she exclaimed, "Sodding hell, and bugger it."

He hid his grin as he stepped out of his truck and said, "Can I give you a hand with those, ma'am?"

The blonde's head snapped up and she shot him a glance over her slim shoulder.

At her sharp look, Mav felt like his stallion, Black Jack, had just delivered a solid kick to his midsection and left him gasping for air.

Impossibly large, slate-blue eyes that were framed by thick dark lashes stared back at him. The woman had come hither, goddess eyes, even with the frown scrunching her brow. Graceful cheekbones in a heart-shaped face, with peaches and cream skin. Full, bow shaped lips that for the life of him, he wanted to see parted in ecstasy, were currently curved-down in displeasure.

This woman wasn't simply attractive, she bordered on an ethereal goddess with her golden beauty. She made him think of fairy maidens and princesses locked in towers, in need of rescuing.

She shifted her beguiling body his way and scrutinized him, planting delicate hands on her shapely hips.

Holy fuck!

His tongue almost lolled out of his mouth. She was slim and curvy in all the right places. But that all dimmed as his gaze stalled during his perusal of her chest. All the blood drained from his head to his groin as he gaped. She had without a doubt one of the finest sets of tits he had ever beheld. The full, rounded globes strained the confines of the sedate ivory blouse covering them, and ignited a pulse-pounding desire in his blood.

The notion of burying his face in the valley between them—or better yet, his dick—blossomed in his mind, and lust slammed his system.

It had been a long time—years, even—since he had met a woman and felt need claw at him. Striding toward her, hell bent on getting to know her in more ways than one, he said, "Here, those look a mite heavy."

She rolled eyes filled with disdain. "Thanks for that, Captain Obvious. I realize that they are heavy, hence the reason why I have yet to remove them from the blasted trunk."

At her haughty reply, he straightened, taking in her measure. Jesus, she might have the body of a fucking goddess but she also had the attitude of an uptight, spoiled brat. "Well, princess, considering it looks like you're attempting to move in with bags that are clearly too heavy for you to manage, why don't you let me get these for ya? And save your breath arguing with me."

She sputtered, "Really, that's not necessary. I don't even know you. For all I know, you could be a total twat and bugger off with everything the moment my back is turned."

Spoiled brat was too nice a term. Clearly, she was high maintenance and needed a lesson in manners—one he would be more than happy to give her. A nice spanking leaving her with a red ass would do it. Her insinuating he was a common criminal pissed him off. "Maverick Greyson; I work for Silver Springs Ranch. And I say my help is warranted, darlin'. The last thing we need is you hurting yourself over stubborn pride because you couldn't accept a helping hand. Now, go on up in the cabin and I'll get these in for you. That way, you won't break a nail or something."

She clenched her hands into fists at her sides, and looked like she wanted to stomp her foot in rage but was holding herself back. Then she opened her mouth to counter him.

Holding up a hand, he cast her an intimidating glare— the same one he used on disobedient subs—and halted the protest before it left her lips. "Don't argue with me, princess. Just do it. This will go a lot faster if you swallow your pride and do as I say."

If anything, her stare turned downright frigid, and she regarded him as if he were something to be scraped off a boot. Her stance was almost regal as she coldly addressed him. "I appreciate the assistance, given there are no bell-hops available on the ranch."

"Seeing as how most people don't pack for an army for a simple vacation in a cabin, bellhops aren't needed," he needled her, and a red blush infused her cheeks.

Her eyes flashed with fury, but she kept her mouth shut. Her response made him want to egg her on just a little bit more; see if he could get a rise out of her. Would her skin flush that way during sex, when she was seconds from climaxing?

Mav was fascinated as she struggled for control and managed to keep her face impassive—except for those goddess eyes. Those blared her emotions.

Jesus, what would they look like with lust clouding them?

With a frustrated sigh, she turned on her heel, strode around the side of the vehicle to the side door, and yanked it open. She fumbled with another suitcase and lifted it out of the back seat. The confounded woman glared with haughty disdain over her small victory, then marched toward the front porch stairs, rolling the tan leather suitcase behind her.

While she struggled hefting the bag up the stairs, Mav just shook his head, bent down, and removed the two large suitcases from the trunk. He grunted, surprised at how heavy they were—not for him, given the scope of his work, but how she thought she could lift them. She had to be a buck twenty dripping wet, and that was only on account of her impressive chest.

He glanced at the luggage tags on the expensive set of bags for a name.

Bianca Peabody out of London, England. That's where the accent came from, and also explained why she had a cultured tone to her crisp alto.

He carted the first set up. His boots clomped on the dark walnut wooden stairs and across the front porch. He left the first two bags just inside the open front door, and then headed back down for the rest.

Seriously, how many damn bags did the woman need for a vacation? Mav had never seen so many, and they affirmed his spoiled brat theory.

He'd have to check registration; find out how long she had the cabin booked for. Mav carted the rest of her belongings in. It didn't take him long. He made sure to close the car doors and trunk before heading in with the last load.

Inside the front door, he assessed her again. "This is the last of it."

She walked over with her wallet in her hand and pulled some cash out. She seemed uneasy with him in her space. She held the cash out toward him and said, "For your troubles. I might have gone overboard with my packing."

He held up a hand. "Not necessary."

"Please take it. You went out of your way and didn't have to. I've been traveling for almost twenty-four hours, and appreciate the help."

Up close, Mav studied her more carefully, and noticed the dark smudges beneath her goddess eyes—eyes that were full of strain and worry. Lust curled in his abdomen—and, startlingly enough, fingers of concern. The Dom in him wanted to wipe away the strain and replace it with pleasure. The man had a feeling that, if he extended his hand, it would be slapped away.

He retreated, taking a step back. "Welcome to Silver Springs Ranch. Be sure to lock the door behind me. I'd rather not have to worry that you were eaten by a mountain lion or got into a brawl with a bear. It'd be bad press for the ranch." He tipped his hat and strode to the door.

She straightened and glanced around like the animals were already inside the cabin. "They wouldn't really come inside, would they?"

"If they're hungry enough or someone antagonizes them, they will, especially if the door isn't locked. And I'm certain in your case, princess, they'd make an exception." He flashed her a grin and wink, then strode out the door without a backward glance.

She was a rather fascinating mix of bluster and fragility —and set his teeth on edge with her condescending disregard.

He didn't know whether he wanted to throttle her or kiss her—possibly both.

But her high-falutin' attitude was enough to make him want to swear off the female species. Because the one thing he was certain of, was that Bianca Peabody would exasperate the dead.

2

*W*ell, that had been a rather epic cock up.

Nice one, really.

Floundering and uncertain, Bianca gaped after the rough cowboy had left, her gaze fixed on the spot where he had stood inside the cabin moments ago.

She was vastly conflicted over the stubborn man.

She hadn't meant to gripe at him. Normally she wasn't that snippy. But her patience had worn thin over twenty-four hours of traveling. Her flight from DC to Denver had been delayed, which had shoved back her departure time from Denver. She probably should have just booked a room in Denver and got a good night's sleep before making the drive—on the wrong side of the bloody road and the wrong side of the sodding car.

But she had pushed through, needing as much distance as possible from her mother and the dreaded state of her future.

Which was why, when the cowboy had come upon her as she had been struggling with the suitcases, frazzled, starving, craving a shower and to go horizontal for twelve solid hours, she had been unable to manage her responses better. Well, that, and because he was a sensual, rugged, handsome manly man who had made every erogenous zone in her body stand up and take notice.

She couldn't be blamed for her actions. The combination had short circuited her control and burned the remaining shreds of her patience. Really, in her defense, when she'd noticed the big black truck parking in front of her cabin like it meant business, her only thought had been: *what now?*

And then the deep, masculine rumble of his voice had asked, "Can I give you a hand with those, ma'am?"

Bianca had swiveled her head in the direction of the voice and been struck dumb.

It had taken all her remaining strength to keep her mouth from falling open with a sigh as she stared at the tall cowboy.

Power radiated off him as he approached. Every inch of him, from his cowboy hat to his boots, blared that this was a man. Not the limp-dicked wimps at the latest charity function or high tea. This man dominated the space he was in. His kinetic energy rolled over her in a lightning strike, and sparked desire in every corner of her body.

Never in her life would she have imagined that denim and plaid could be a sexy combination, and make her consider wanting to climb the man in question like he was a tree. But when it came to the cowboy, considering the way the jeans fit his powerful thighs, it did.

Unable to do anything but stare at him, she had surveyed his rough-hewn features, and his impossibly wide shoulders encased in the plaid blue shirt that strained over firm muscles. The cuffs had been rolled up near his elbows, displaying powerfully muscled forearms and a set of big, strong hands that made her wonder how they would feel on her skin.

But it had been his face, shadowed by the black Stetson atop his head, that had garnered the bulk of her attention. He had a strong, angular jaw, and pronounced cheekbones that added to his rough stance. His face was harsh and distinctly male, with its blunt angles. His nose was slightly crooked, like it had been broken a time or two. His eyes were pools of liquid gold amber, framed by thick, dark brows. The dark umber five o'clock shadow shrouded a kissable set of lips. And those lips had been curled at the ends in a lopsided grin as he approached her.

That potent, engaging grin made whatever brain cells she'd had left after her long day of traveling implode as her body heated from the inside out. Her attraction to the stranger had both stirred her up and made her livid. She hadn't flown halfway around the globe to avoid marrying one man, just to hop into bed with another. Nor had she missed the way his eyes came to a shuddering halt at her chest. Yes, she had great boobs. But there seemed to be this assumption by men that because she was blessed in that area, she was automatically willing to join them in bed, as if her sizable rack made her an easy tumble.

After that, there had been no stopping the words that came flying out of her mouth.

Bollocks!

Nothing like letting it all go to pot with an employee of the ranch. It put a cherry on top of a crappy week. The next time she ran into him, she would apologize for her behavior. Considering she had booked the cabin for five weeks, she would rather stop a war before it started.

Bianca knew the kerfuffle with the cowboy had been her fault, just like the sad state of the rest of her life.

Her mobile chose that moment to ring, with her mum's name flashing on the screen. *See, barely twenty-four hours of respite before the woman started hounding me.* Bianca declined the call, letting the sodding thing go to voicemail like the other four times.

The nicest part about hiding out in a cabin five thousand miles from home was that she could ignore her mum's summons. She wouldn't have to worry about her stopping by to check up on her, when Bianca preferred to stay in. Here in the breathtaking Rockies, far removed from everyone and everything she knew, Bianca could just be herself for a change, and perhaps even remember who she wanted to be. Do the things that she wanted, and not what she must do in order to uphold the family name. On the ranch, and in the nearby town of Winter Park, no one cared about her exalted lineage—she was a descendant of the Plantagenets—or whether she was making the right match, or whether she had perpetrated a faux pas that would follow her family name for generations.

When a banner popped up on her phone announcing a new voicemail, she rolled her eyes. She needed wine, some food, and to go horizontal for twelve hours.

And then she would see. For once in her life, she wasn't making any plans.

She surveyed the cabin itself and took a walk through it to get a feel for the place she would be calling home for the next few weeks. The lodge was charming with its golden honey-toned wood walls and vaulted ceiling. She picked the larger of the two bedrooms and rolled her numerous suitcases into the room, stowing them against a wall until tomorrow. There was a generous king mattress that looked like a lovely cloud of relaxation, piled with pillows and with a Western patterned beige and blue quilt spread over the top. The room also had a full dresser, and there was an attached bath. The bathroom was a thing of beauty, in tones of deep blue and gold. There was a tiled shower stall, and a deep-seated dark blue tub with jacuzzi jets.

On her next foray into town, she would have to pick up supplies for a bubble bath.

The second bedroom was a mite smaller, but it had its own bath as well, though the room she had chosen was more impressive.

Glad she had made that decision, Bianca plodded back down the hall. The main area of the cabin was an open floor plan without any walls between the living, dining area, and kitchen. Going into the kitchen, she stored the groceries she had picked up in town before she reached the ranch.

On autopilot, she made a light dinner that consisted of a slice of the crusty French bread, some cheese slices, and she also cut up an apple, and added a few slices of the prosciutto and some baby carrots. The bottle of pinot grigio wasn't chilled, but after the day she'd had and the incessant buzzing on her phone from her mother's multitude of calls, Bianca poured a glass of wine into one of the glass tumblers supplied in the cabin.

She ate her dinner standing at the kitchen counter. It was freeing not to have to answer to a soul for a change.

She figured her mother would fume for the first two weeks she was absent. Her father would follow along with whatever her mum dictated, since she ruled the roost with an iron fist. And Peter would simply assume Bianca had taken off on a holiday to a spa somewhere like in the Swiss Alps to refresh herself.

Now that she was here and felt like she could take a deep breath for the first time in forever, she didn't know if she could go back. Which was rubbish. Of course she would return to London at the end of her stay... wouldn't she?

By the time her belly was satiated, the long hours of travel had her body drooping. Rinsing the empty plate and glass in the sink, she figured she would wash them in the morning. Fighting back a yawn, she trudged back down the hall, shutting off lights as she went.

In the bedroom, she didn't even bother to locate her pajamas. No one was going to see her or care if she slept with no clothes on. She brushed her teeth with the toothbrush and paste stored in the travel kit she pulled from her handbag, then stripped down to her panties, tossing her clothing on top of her suitcases, and crawled beneath the covers.

Bianca didn't even set the alarm. She cuddled under the warm blankets, and closed her eyes. She was out in under five minutes.

3

*M*onday morning dawned early after his day off. Up before the sun crested the craggy outline of the mountains, Maverick Greyson had work coming out his ears. As the Head Wrangler for Silver Springs Ranch, it was his job to stay on top of all the animals on the ranch and manage the wranglers' work schedules. They had both year-round full-time workers and seasonal wranglers in their crew. The seasonal bunch were typically college kids home for the summer, looking to make some extra cash. The ranch could certainly use the help, as busy as they tended to get in the summer. But all year long, Mav's job kept him engaged from sun up to sundown.

In addition to the cattle drives they hosted for guests to get a taste of what it was like being a cowboy on the range, they also hosted trail rides, overnight camping excursions, overnight cattle drives, and offered survivalist training with Duncan.

They also had cookouts and barbecues, campfire nights, and square dances in the ballroom of the hotel.

There was rarely a dull moment in ranch life, especially

given that this was a tourist destination as well as a working dude ranch. They had to mind the visitors and, at times, protect the animals from them.

Mav worked closely with the ranch horse master, Noah, to maintain the schedule on the horse rotations on the hundreds owned by the ranch. His buddy Tanner had moved up in the ranks since Emmett had pulled back on operating the overnight cattle drives all the time after getting hitched this past winter. It was on account of Emmett's lady love, the town doc, Grace, he was taking the extra time and wanted his nights back.

Not that Mav blamed Emmett one bit—if he had a sweet woman who looked like Grace waiting at home for him, he would want the time with her too. If he was that kind of man. Settling down was fine for some guys—his friends Emmett and Colt had taken to it right fine.

But Mav didn't believe he was the settling down type himself. For some, it worked, and for others, it ended up being a prison with no escape. Besides, there was such an available bounty of women who tended to throw themselves his way.

How could he refuse?

That train of thought brought to mind the spoiled brat he had helped the other night. She'd been a damn looker. Blonde, slim, with breasts that made him want to weep for joy at the female form, and a snooty attitude that made him itch to draw her over his damn knee to teach her some respect.

All of that launched a world of possibilities when it came to what he could do with her between the sheets. It was sad to admit that she had starred in a few of his fantasies over the last two nights. All the naughty things he could do with those glorious tits—even the simple thought of the way they would jiggle as he pumped inside her—made his gut clench. Although, with the mouth she had on her, he would likely have to amend some of those erotic visions to include a ball gag.

Jesus, he couldn't think of her that way. He didn't even know whether he liked the British chick—not that that had ever stopped him from taking a woman to bed.

He checked on reports from wranglers, checked in with forest rangers for a count and update on local predator movement, and scoured through data on the current snow melt and thawing. It was May, which meant they could have three days of gorgeous eighty-degree temps, and then have a sudden snowstorm barrel in, dump two feet of white powder and make weather conditions plummet below freezing, only for it to thaw out by the end of the week and turn the trails into thick rivers of mud.

Just because it snowed, that didn't mean they got the day off, not with the responsibilities they had with the horses and cows. But that was why he checked on forecasts, and studied their supply numbers on feed for the horses and cattle. And while they did their best to let the cattle graze mainly on grass, during the winter months it was damn hard to do, so they supplemented the animals' diet with cattle feed then.

Mav also had to double check that the horse feed and cow feed did not get mixed up. They had different storage lockers for the stables and cattle pens when the animals were stuck in the barns. He knew that some people didn't like cows being stuck in a small space in a barn for months on end. But it was better than them freezing to death when there was three feet of snow on the ground, and it was below zero out. They had outdoor corrals, so the animals weren't inside all the time.

He needed to saddle up in a bit, and go check on some of the high-country fences. One of the wranglers had reported a herd of elk had passed through and taken out part of the fencing. While Silver Springs was a dude ranch, as a working ranch, it had the same needs and problems as a regular ranch.

Carrying his tack and saddle towards Black Jack's stall, Mav picked up the distinct sound of a British accent near the front desk. It must be their newest guest from across the pond. He settled the tack and saddle over Jack's stall door. Jack peered at him with impatience to be out on the range.

"Be back in a moment, bud." He rubbed his stallion's inky nose and headed out to see what the commotion was at the front.

Mav squinted as he stepped outside while his gaze adjusted to the sunlight. And there she stood, talking with Trevor, one of their seasonal workers who had been with them three summers running. Trevor was studying to be a forest ranger. His time here would serve him well.

What the hell was she wearing?

The woman was dressed in riding gear that was more suited to afternoon tea than to riding the range in Colorado. Granted, the beige pants displayed her slim, toned legs to perfection, and Mav couldn't help but admire the way they fit. He doubted he had ever seen black riding boots that were that clean, without a scuff in place. The ivory long-sleeved shirt and protective black vest hugged the curves of her generous cleavage. That long blonde hair had been pulled back and lay in a thick braid over one shoulder.

He could imagine wrapping that braid in his hand to hold her in place as he took her from behind. Jesus, he needed to get a grip. The sudden onslaught of lust mixed with his anger.

The quip left his mouth before he could stop it. "That's what you're planning to wear horse riding, princess?"

"It's perfectly acceptable." Her sultry blue eyes slanted in his direction. Her delicate features were schooled in a prim, dismissive manner, like she was staring at shit that needed to be scraped off boots.

"If you say so, princess. Ever ridden a horse?" he asked derisively, looking her up and down. The woman didn't look strong enough to handle a horse, but he also was well aware that looks could be deceiving.

"Plenty, on the English saddle. However, I never had the chance to learn on a Western style saddle, and would like to," she replied haughtily.

He studied her, rather surprised. It meant she had some skills. "I can teach you."

"But I don't want you," she said dismayed, apparently rather horrified at the possibility.

Didn't she realize that her response gave him all the fuel he needed? He was a perverse creature and a bit of a sadist. Causing her discomfort that wouldn't really harm her would satisfy him on a twisted level that was right up his alley. "Princess, it's not a matter of what you want, it's what I'm willing to give. Take it or leave it."

Trevor adjusted his white Stetson and said, "Ah, Mav—"

Mav cut the younger wrangler off and noted the gleam of interest in the kid's eyes. She would eat the poor bastard alive and stomp on his heart on the way out the door. No, this one required a firmer hand than the boy had. "I've got this, Trevor. Why don't you go saddle Sunshine for me and bring her out? That way, I can get a feel for the princess's skills."

Trevor glanced longingly at the woman for a minute,

before he nodded at Mav and strode inside to fetch Sunshine.

"There's no reason to be rude," she stated primly once Trevor was out of earshot.

Christ, she did something to Mav with that haughty stare. He let her understand who was boss with a single glare, one that normally made submissives quiver. But not Miss Peabody—she challenged him with a defiant glimmer.

"My place, my rules. I run the stables. If you don't like it, you don't have to ride. How long have you been riding for?" He assessed her with an eye toward leg length, trying to determine how she would sit on a saddle. He'd been doing this long enough with tourists that usually he knew the moment he spied the person. But with Miss Prim and Proper, he couldn't get a feel for her and how she would take to the saddle.

She huffed. "Since I was old enough to sit in a saddle. All through primary and secondary school, I competed, show jumping. Until I went away to university and didn't have time for such frivolities."

His brows rose. Horse riding a frivolity? That was a five-dollar word for a pastime. And while he'd not expected her to have any real talent, her words gave him pause.

Trevor appeared with Sunshine, a sweet, mild mannered, six-year-old, spotted Appaloosa who was eager to please her riders.

"Thanks, Trevor. Follow me, princess." Mav jerked his chin in the direction of the paddock as he took the reins from the wrangler.

"Really, I don't see what all the fuss is about. I just want to learn to ride on the Western saddle."

"This is so I can get a feel for your skill level, and how much work will be required. I'm a busy man and don't have all day to cater to your whims." What Mav didn't say was that it was normally his pal, Noah, horse master extraordinaire, who did the riding lessons around the ranch. Well, he and his staff, but Mav was perverse enough to want to handle this one himself.

She rolled her eyes. "Are you this well-mannered with all the guests?"

With Sunshine standing still, waiting for her rider to mount, Maverick threaded his hands together and bent a little, since Miss Peabody really was a small thing, to help her mount without a mounting block. "Nope, I'm like this especially for you. I don't have time to grab the block. Hands on my shoulders, and I'll give you a boost."

With her jaw set, she placed delicate hands on his shoulders. Electric currents zapped through him at her innocent touch, coursing from his shoulders all the way to his boot heels. She set her foot in his hands. He lifted her up and she swung her leg over the saddle. She didn't fumble around like some tourists did the first moment they mounted a horse. Once she was seated, he adjusted the stirrups to fit her shorter legs, double checking that everything was cinched and in place.

Handing her the reins, he ordered, "Take her for a slow walk around the paddock; let me see what I'll have to work with."

She pinned him with a frosty glare, and adjusted herself in the seat, like she was getting a feel for the leather. Reins in hand, she kicked her heels and flicked the reins, giving Sunshine the signal to move.

The two started off around the ring.

The woman rode like a queen—poised, precise and, by the end of their trot around the ring, Sunshine was damn near purring with delight at her rider. Mav couldn't help but feel a sexual pull in her direction. Any man worth his salt would look at the way she commanded the mare, in full control as they trotted around the pen, and wonder if she would give them as good a ride.

When horse and rider returned to his side, there was an imperious gleam of victory in her gaze. He nodded. "You'll do. Be here at seven a.m. tomorrow."

Lifting her up, he plucked her off Sunshine's back. There was a brief moment where their bodies collided before he set her on her feet. It was a simple graze, nothing more, but his body sizzled from the slight contact. He released her like he had stuck his hand in a branding fire.

"In the morning?" she sputtered, and stared up at him like he was crazy.

His lips curled up in a devious grin. "We're not all royalty, princess. Around here, the day starts before the sun rises. If you want lessons on the Western saddle, that's when I'm available."

"But surely there must be someone else." She didn't say besides him, but those words were clearly written across her face, with her lush lips turned down in displeasure and the scowl marring her forehead.

"There's not. Take it or leave it. Doesn't really matter one way or the other to me." He shrugged with a blasé stare. Maverick wasn't sure why ruffling her stiff feathers gave him such a sadistic thrill, but it did. As a Dom, he thoroughly enjoyed doling out punishment when and where it was necessary.

"Fine. I will be here," she replied through clenched teeth.

Gripping Sunshine's reins, he nodded and started to walk back toward the stables but then glanced mockingly over his shoulder and said, "Oh, and princess? Wear a damn pair of jeans, and not that fancy get up."

Maverick strode back into the stables leading Sunshine, and handed her off to another wrangler before heading toward Black Jack's stall. He whistled as he saddled his horse. If Miss Peabody wanted to step into the boxer's ring and go a few contentious rounds with him, he was game.

And he would win.

4

*T*hat bloody cowboy!

Bianca stomped back to her cabin, riding a wave of fury that could level the nearby mountains. Who did that neanderthal think he was to treat her this way?

She slammed the cabin door behind her. If he wanted her to wear jeans, she would go and buy some bloody jeans. She didn't have any on account of her mother insisting her wardrobe needed sprucing up last spring. Her mum had torn through Bianca's wardrobe, donating what she felt her daughter had outgrown or was too important to be seen wearing.

Hence her lack of available blue jeans.

Removing her riding outfit, she changed into a pair of trousers and a blouse. At least she hadn't worn her riding helmet—Maverick would have mocked her about it. Studying her available shoe collection, she went with a pair of nude flats. Glancing in the mirror, she appraised her reflection and outfit.

Nice one, really.

Maverick wasn't wrong about her appearance. Who

wore trousers and flats on a ranch? Just because she had left London, didn't mean she looked different. And the horse stables she had attended as a child looked like an ostentatious palace where the Queen had afternoon tea.

It was time to change her normal dress code—not radically, but enough so that her mother's influence didn't flavor her clothing choices. Maybe she would purchase a few more items besides jeans. If the local shops didn't have exactly what she wanted, perhaps she would drive to Denver in a day or so, when she felt recovered from her travels. A city that size would certainly have plenty of shops.

Ready for the trip into Winter Park, with her handbag and keys in hand, Bianca headed out to the sedan she had rented. Glancing at the other cabins down the lane, she noticed trucks and sport utility vehicles parked out in front.

Even her choice of rental car, the black Mercedes, made her stick out.

She drove off the ranch property. In the light of day, the scenery she had missed in the darkening twilight when she'd arrived two nights ago left her in awe. It was stunning. Breathtaking. The steep, jagged peaks, some covered with glaciers. The way the land sloped and rolled, covered in deep evergreen pines, which were such vibrant slashes of color against the vivid blue sky, dotted with puffy white clouds. The scene made her ache to pick up a sketch pad and draw the surrounding area—maybe even paint it.

Inside her, there was a sudden spurt of happiness that shocked through her system. The thought of painting, of creating again, relaxed her being far more than anything else. There had to be a place she could order supplies online and have them delivered. She would check at the registration desk when she returned, ask about getting packages delivered to the ranch.

In the quaint, picturesque town of Winter Park, she found a parking spot not far from the main hub of shops at Cooper Creek Square. The small municipality charmed her with its appearance. Strolling through the square, she located a boutique that sold women's clothing where she picked up jeans, less formal tops, socks, a less formal outdoor jacket and a hat. It wasn't a cowboy hat, but a cute sun bucket one that would keep the sun out of her eyes on hikes or out riding.

Luck was on her side for a change. Two doors down from the clothing shop was a shoe store. She picked up a pair of hiking boots, some tennis shoes, and riding boots that might possibly make the idiot cowboy sneer at her less.

Not that it mattered what he thought of her.

Except the sight of him this morning, in his milieu at the stables, had churned her up inside. She didn't like the lout. He was rude and uncouth. And yet, his frustrating behavior mattered very little to her hormones. Those pesky bastards took one look at his coarse exterior in plaid and denim, covered with dust, and batted their damn lashes his way.

This morning, when she'd used him as her mounting block and touched him, laid her palms on those wide, muscled shoulders, heat had deluged her system. It had overwhelmed her, made her tongue tied, and long to touch him without his shirt on. Would the burn flay the skin from her hands?

His rangy, powerfully built body was potent and wickedly sinful, all while his mocking gaze called her ten times a fool for choosing the ranch as the place to hide herself away.

Secretly, Bianca had hoped that if she visited a location where no one knew her, she wouldn't stand out, and would fit in. Although everyone she had met—with Maverick being the exception—had been nice. Perhaps, at the heart of it, she needed to quit caring what other people thought of her, and focus instead on the way she felt about herself.

Because, truthfully, she abhorred what she had become. That was at the root of all her disquiet and malaise, the panic and dread at following through with the wedding. In the years since she'd graduated university, she had become almost Stepford like in thought and deed, always catering to others, especially her mum, and changing herself to accommodate them, instead of being who she was at her core.

Most days, she didn't recognize the woman in the mirror. But that would change. It had to; *she* had to remove all the fake layers she had assumed and piled on to survive, and burn them to the fucking ground.

Because that last little sliver of her true being was gasping for oxygen, clinging to life. And it terrified Bianca to think what would happen if she allowed that sliver to be snuffed out.

She didn't like herself all that much. She hated her life —which made her feel like the worst person ever. Moaning and bitching about the state of her existence when she had never wanted for a thing. Except, she was miserable. If she had to attend one more tea where all the ladies present gossiped like a bunch of hens, and pretended the little sandwiches and micro salads were enough food to satisfy them, when she knew they would subsequently head into the bathroom and throw it all up in their efforts to remain thin, she would lose the last vestiges of her sanity.

"Bloody hell."

"Sorry, is everything all right?" the young clerk asked as she rang up Bianca's purchases. The girl couldn't be older than eighteen. She still had that sweet baby face, with no hint of crow's feet on her freckled skin.

"It's nothing. I've needed this holiday for a long time," Bianca explained with a forced smile.

"Well, we're glad you chose our tiny little town for your destination. Say, are you from England?" the girl asked, her inky ponytail shifting as she tilted her head and stared with interest.

"I am." Bianca nodded, feeling the eyes of the other shoppers look her way. Being in the spotlight and the center of attention made her want to melt into the carpet just to get away.

"That's so cool! Do you know Prince William and the royal family?"

"We're cousins, but I don't know him well," Bianca blurted out, then felt her face flame at the clerk's loud gasp.

"You're related to them? How awesome!" she exclaimed with curious excitement bubbling out of her.

"It's really not all that interesting, I can assure you." Bianca took her credit card back from the clerk and collected her bags. She guessed that, from the outside looking in, the archaic institutions of the aristocracy and royal family seemed fascinating. While she did like how far back her family could be traced, and knowing who some of her ancestors were, she hated all the pomp and circumstance surrounding it.

Wildly aware of all the eyes staring at her over her admission, she hightailed it from the shop.

Bollocks!

Bianca had come to Colorado to hide. Why the hell had she admitted the relationship? They were distant cousins—like a five times removed sort of thing.

Nice one. She'd stuck her foot in her mouth once more. What was one more embarrassment to add to the list and make her entire escape go to pot? This was a prime example of why she had such a hard time fitting in. She always spoke her mind, and didn't filter her words enough. There seemed to be a disconnect between her brain and her mouth.

Beyond embarrassed, Bianca prayed no one from the shoe store was following her to snap a picture that they would post on social media. She could imagine the sodding caption: *Prince William's cousin spotted in America.*

Walking quickly, her hands loaded with bags, she darted inside a store when she thought one of the shoppers was following her—and stopped dead in her tracks. Her gaze roved over the shelves and displays.

It was fantastic. A dream, really, that she had stumbled upon this place. That the shop existed amidst the tee shirt and tourist junk shops. This was her nirvana. A fully equipped art store. Bianca felt a door inside her rattle. Her fingers flexed, holding the bags. The need to pick up brush and pencil. The urgent desire to run her fingers over canvas almost brought her to her knees.

"Welcome. Can I help you find anything?" the older gentleman asked as he cleaned his spectacles on his shirt.

"Your shop is wonderful," Bianca replied, taking it all in. Shopping here was going to be better than a sale at Harrods.

"Thank you kindly, miss. Do you like art?" He settled his glasses back on his face.

"I love it." Standing in there, the smell of the art supplies brought a multitude of memories swarming back into her psyche—of the time in her life when she had rebelled, and fed the demands of her soul. She wanted to open a tube of oil paint and breathe the aroma in.

"Well, we have all the supplies you might want or need, to create. What do you like to do?"

"Paint. But it's been a while. Could I leave my bags

with you while I look around?"

"Certainly. I can put them right behind the counter here for you. And let me know if you need any help."

She smiled at him—what she was sure was her first, real genuine smile in months—and handed the gentlemen her shopping haul. "Thank you."

Bianca started in the aisle with the sketch books and loaded her arms up with multiple sizes. This way, she could stuff one in the hiking sack she'd picked up and it wouldn't take up too much space. In the next row, she grabbed packages of pencils, charcoal, sharpening tools, and colored pencils. When her arms were full, she headed to the counter with her load.

"Is that all for you today?" the kind gentleman asked.

"No. This is just the first stack." She watched dollar signs appear in the man's blue eyes.

He took the pile from her. "No problem at all, miss. I'll set these right back here on the shelf for you."

And then she was off again. She spent time in the aisle with the paint brushes, selecting all the different brushes she used to like to work with. There were color palettes to hold paint colors on an endcap, and she grabbed two. This way, if the mood struck right after she'd finished one painting, she could move on to the next seamlessly. There were packages of drop cloths she added to protect the cabin's hardwood floor. Then an adjustable wooden H frame studio easel. It would work best if she wanted to shift sizes on the different canvases. Struggling with her second load, she carried it to the front.

The man behind the counter just raised his bushy silver brows, a smile playing on his lips as he added those items to her growing pile behind the register.

The man probably thought she was insane or having a

breakdown.

But thoughts of the clerk fled as she loaded up on paint: oils, acrylics, and watercolors. Her favorite was oil. But while she was here and exploring who she wanted to be, it was time to experiment to her heart's content. She wanted to try a few different pouring mediums, color pigments, and types of paint. Then she moved on to selecting canvas. The store had plenty of premade canvases that would get her started. It had been years since she had crafted her own frame and stretched canvas over it—not since she had apprenticed with a master in Italy.

Yet she wanted to do it, wanted the workspace where she could cut and mold the wooden frame.

By the time she'd finished shopping and taken stock of her haul, she knew there was no way it would all fit in her car. "You wouldn't deliver by any chance, would you?"

The clerk was happily ringing up her purchases and grinned broadly. "Of course; I can schedule that for tomorrow. I don't have the extra help today, though, if you need it all right away."

"Tomorrow would be great. I just want to take the sketchbooks and pencils with me. The rest can be delivered. I'm staying at one of the cabins over at Silver Springs Ranch for the next few weeks."

"It's a lovely stretch of land. And with all this, you'll be quite busy."

She hid her wince when he gave her the total. It wasn't every day she spent more than four thousand dollars on art supplies. But in her defense, she was starting from scratch. Master Renaud would tut and shake his head at her if he knew how many years it had been since she had picked up a paint brush.

That changed now.

5

*B*ianca left Archie's Art Supply store with a miniscule portion of her shopping haul today, and realized she was famished. She stopped at a lovely café with outdoor seating. After an indulgent lunch filled with carbs, she headed to her car with her bags and loaded them in the boot. On the drive back, she visited the grocery store. Due to how tired she had been when she had arrived on Saturday night, she had only grabbed a few basics. This way, she would have things on hand to eat. Although there was a restaurant on the ranch grounds that she had yet to try. Perhaps she should do that for dinner tonight. There was a liquor store right next to the grocer. She bought more wine and a few bottles of scotch, rather pleased with their selection.

There was even an American brand of whiskey she chose to add to the bunch that was from Meath Irish Distillery right there in Colorado.

Basically, by the time she had finished shopping in Winter Park, she had done her part and contributed to the local economy. Thank heavens she could afford it.

When she arrived back at the ranch, she stopped by the main hotel and went inside. She wanted to use the spare bedroom in the cabin as an art studio during her stay. But that meant having the furniture in the room moved out of the way.

At the registration counter, Jessica, the petite, brunette clerk Bianca had met when she checked in Saturday, was there, and smiled. "Miss Peabody, how are you enjoying your stay so far?"

"Great, I had a lovely afternoon in the shops in Winter Park. I was wondering... would there be a way to move the furniture out of the spare bedroom?"

Tilting her head, Jessica grimaced. "I'm not sure. Is there something you don't like about the cabin? Perhaps we can see if there's another one that would suit you better."

"Oh no, the cabin is great. It's just, I was hoping to turn the spare room into a bit of an art studio while I'm here. And I didn't know if it would be possible to move the bed— and perhaps the dresser out of the way."

"Let me make a quick call," Jessica said, and picked up the phone with a pensive expression.

Not a minute later, a stunning woman in a simple black suit and killer set of heels appeared at the counter.

"Miss Peabody, I'm Amber Anderson, the owner of Silver Springs Ranch," she said, and extended a hand.

She accepted and shook her hand. "Bianca, please."

"Bianca, I was hoping to meet you at some point, since you've rented the cabin for the next five weeks. We don't normally have guests stay longer than a week or two. Now, Jessica tells me that you want some furniture moved in the spare bedroom?"

Bianca twisted her hands. "Yes. If it's not too much trouble. I was going to turn it into a bit of an art studio while

I'm here. I have drop cloths and everything to protect the hardwood floor. And will even put a bigger deposit down to cover the room. That way, if anything should end up damaged, the deposit would cover it for you."

Amber studied her for a moment. "I think we can accommodate you. When would you need the items moved?"

"Well, I'm having a bunch of supplies delivered tomorrow from Archie's Art Supplies. There's no huge rush. If it takes a few days, that's all right," Bianca said, although her platitudes were bullshit. She fancied having the space made available as soon as possible—mainly because she feared the bubbling font of need coursing through her to pick up a paint brush and splash color onto canvas again, would flee.

Bianca's emotions walked on a tightrope: one wrong move, and she would tumble into darkness for all eternity.

"Let me see what I can do to get those items moved for you tonight. Just the bed and dresser in the room, yes?" Amber asked, for confirmation.

"Yes, the nightstands with the lights can stay. I hate to be an imposition and would be happy to pay for moving them out and then back in," Bianca said.

Amber held up a hand. "How about you tip the movers for their trouble tonight, since it will be outside their normal duties? I'll add a two-hundred-dollar deposit onto your account—of which you will get back fifty percent at the end of your stay—to help cover the cost of manpower moving the furniture back in. Is that acceptable?"

"Yes, more than. I love your shoes by the way. Louboutins?" Bianca nodded at the black leather heels with sheer black mesh and silver spikes.

Amber quirked a brow. "Good eye. Let me make a few

calls. I will get some of my guys over there by seven tonight. Does that work for you?"

"Absolutely. Thank you so much."

"You should join me for lunch sometime while you're here. If you can spot Louboutins that easily, I'm sure we have a lot in common." Amber smiled.

"That would be nice." It amazed Bianca that this confident businesswoman lived in the rustic mountains, and was extending an offer of possible friendship over a shared love of shoes.

"I'll contact you later in the week and we'll set something up." Amber checked her watch. "If you don't have movers there by seven, call my cell phone and I will get on the horn." She jotted her number down on a business card and handed it over.

"I appreciate it. And will let you get back to work."

As she strode out of the main building, Bianca felt good. Hell, she felt great, as if a two-ton elephant had been lifted from her shoulders.

The prospect of painting, the possibility of making a new friend—one who wasn't aware of her societal status—even learning to ride on the Western saddle with the rough cowboy as her instructor, infused her entire system with an emotion she'd thought had long since fled her existence and vocabulary.

Hope.

Hope that her future might not be the boring cycle of endless repetition, with the same tedious people who were all vying to outdo one another in a never-ending loop of social gatherings.

Hope that her life might hold possibilities for a different path. One that fed her soul and filled her with peace instead of crippling anxiety and dread.

Back at her cabin, Bianca carted her purchases inside and stowed them away. Then she tackled her luggage. Since she was staying for five weeks, there was no reason to keep her clothing in her suitcases. She unpacked case after case. She even had to go into the spare room to grab more hangers —to her unending shame. On her next trip to the market, she would pick up a few more hangers. But otherwise, she was set up nicely.

She unloaded her toiletries, storing them in the vanity drawers, and arranged the bathroom for ease of use.

When she'd finished those tasks, she headed into the spare room and stripped the bedding. She folded the sheets and stored them on the shelves in the closet. She had just slid the closet door closed when a loud, pounding knock thudded against the front door.

Bianca walked to the front door, floating on breezy happiness. She opened the heavy oak door with a smile on her face, but it froze in place the moment she spied the bloody cowboy on the porch.

"Princess." The big rangy cowboy, Maverick, tipped his hat. Those golden eyes assessed her from head to toe. Heat curled in her belly.

"What are you doing here?" she asked, her spine stiffening as she fought the desire to put her hand back on his shoulder.

He cocked a dark brow. "As far as I know, we're here to move some furniture out for you."

We?

Maverick shifted on his feet and she finally caught a glimpse of the cowboy behind him. The unknown cowboy was blond like her, with an engaging smile, and just as tall as his friend.

"Ma'am, it's nice to meet you. I'm Tanner, and I see

you've already met Maverick. Amber mentioned that you were needing the space. We should be able to get it all in one trip." He nodded to the two big trucks parked outside the cabin.

"Um, yes, won't you come in? I already removed the bed linen," she explained, feeling like she was fumbling as she glanced at Maverick again.

The two cowboys wiped their boots on the outdoor mat before stepping inside. Suddenly, Bianca's cabin was suffused with oodles of testosterone. These weren't dandies pontificating at the club after a polo match. These were rugged, testosterone-laden men, and they made no apologies for who they were.

While Tanner was a gorgeous specimen with his golden looks, he didn't hold a candle to Maverick, or cause her entire body to tighten and pulse with need, like Maverick's nearness did.

Ignoring the wild fluttering in her stomach, she strode down the hall, the men's heavy footsteps following behind her. At the doors to the rooms, she gestured to the smaller one. "It's this one."

"What do you plan to do with the room? Need more room for your luggage?" Maverick asked drolly, letting her know that he considered her nothing but a piece of fluff.

"I was thinking more along the lines of a sex dungeon," she commented with a shrug, her voice dripping with sarcasm.

Both cowboys' eyebrows rose at the offhand response. Tanner laughed and winked at her. "Well, I would be happy to be your first victim—um, partner—if that's the case."

"I'll keep that in mind."

"Sex dungeon?" Maverick inspected her, his gaze roving

up and down her form like he was taking her measure. "You don't have it in you."

"You don't know me well enough to make that evaluation. But if you really must know, I will be using this room as an art studio during my stay. My supplies will be here tomorrow."

"So you're an artist?" Tanner asked, appearing interested.

He was rather adorable. Maybe she did need to have some hot sex while she was here. But the instant she thought that, her brain and body conjured the man who was swiftly becoming the bane of her existence. "I dabble. Why do you ask?"

"Well, if you need a model, I would be happy to assist. I'd even pose nude, if that's your type of thing." Tanner was laying the innuendo on thick.

Bianca could appreciate him. He was handsome and forthright. And friendly, which was more than she could say for the other one. That one—his dark sensuality made her desire naughty, wicked acts she had no business contemplating, and he also made her want to do him bodily harm.

"If you could quit flirting with the princess, we can get this stuff moved out faster."

"It's Bianca, not princess. I'll let you gentlemen handle this, as I'm sure I haven't the foggiest idea how to move this stuff out properly."

"We've got you covered, Bianca," Tanner said with a friendly smile.

Maverick just leveled her with a frank stare. Like he could see through all her pretenses, past the face she wore, to the very heart of her being—and found her lacking. It hit far too close to home. And it spurred her into retreating into the living room. She withdrew cash from her purse to hand them when they were finished, and laid it on the kitchen counter.

Needing something—anything to do, really, she opened a bottle of wine and poured herself a glass. There was no way she was getting through the next twenty minutes without a drink.

She really was rather hopeless when it came to the kitchen. But that was why she had picked up some ready-made meals. The two cowboys carted the mattress and box springs out to the trucks like they weighed nothing. There was some deliberation, as they took the wooden bed apart, on how best to fit it in the truck with the dresser.

Through it all, every time they passed, Bianca locked gazes with Maverick, then experienced a deep blast of energy that was three parts desire, one part fury. She couldn't be attracted to the big lout. If she was, then she had really driven off the deep end.

What had she been thinking, joking with them about a sex dungeon? Who said stuff like that? She did, apparently, which was what made appearances at the charity events and polo matches so much fun. She would speak, and heads would turn—and not in a good way. More in a: *can you believe that came out of her mouth?* sort of way.

"Bianca, we're all finished. We even rolled up the rug and stored it in the closet for you. So be careful if you open those doors," Tanner said with a smile, standing near the front door.

"We'll get out of your hair, princess," Maverick said.

"Wait," she said, grabbing the tip off the counter. She handed Tanner and Maverick the cash. Maverick's fingers connected with hers, and she sucked in a breath at the livewire that flash-fried her nerve endings. Her gaze shot his way, needing to see if he had felt the jolt as well.

But the dratted man merely stared, like he had her number and wasn't impressed.

"Well hells bells, I'm heading into town and getting a steak dinner with this. Thanks," Tanner exclaimed. "Would you like to join me?"

His sweet offer hung in the air, with Maverick glaring at him as if he had lost his mind. As much as Bianca might like to stick it to the cowboy, she wasn't interested in going anywhere this evening.

"I appreciate the offer, Tanner, truly. It's been a long day, and I'm still experiencing some jet lag. Thank you both for your help this evening," she said with small smile.

"Perhaps another time then," Tanner stated with clear interest in his green gaze.

"Maybe." She held the front door open as they filed outside.

"If you need anything, come find me at the stables. I'm happy to help with whatever you might require," Tanner offered.

"Don't forget, seven a.m., princess," Maverick stated, his face impassive.

"I'll be there," she replied grimly, and shut the door. There was the heavy stomping of their boots over the porch, and then the truck engines igniting. She sighed. Thank goodness they were gone. Another few minutes around Maverick, and she would have made an utter fool of herself.

Bianca didn't know what it was about Maverick that really pushed all her hot buttons, other than he accomplished it with startling ease.

$\mathcal{T}$he loud buzzing of the bedside alarm clock had Bianca glaring menacingly at the contraption. Six fifteen in the blasted morning. It was a ghastly time to be awake. And she realized how spoiled she was to be thinking that.

But it was godawful.

Whoever had begun the tradition of starting the day before sunrise should be whipped. Bianca preferred tea most mornings, but to handle being up this early, only the brash infusion of coffee would do.

As the coffee brewed, she dressed in her modified riding outfit. Instead of the beige breeches, she wore jeans and the new riding boots. Temperatures were chilly this morning, making her shiver as she dressed. She donned a light jacket to stave off the wind and keep her warm. After downing the coffee, she grabbed an apple from the fruit bowl she had set on the counter, to eat for breakfast on the way to the stables. Whatever she didn't finish, she would give to the horse.

Or she could throw it at the cowboy's head if he was being an ass.

Either way, she would get double uses out of the fruit.

When she stepped outside the cabin, she wasn't prepared for the spectacular light show of dawn hitting the mountains. The profusion of golds, bright bold oranges bleeding into pink, red, and then purple as the inky indigo sky retreated, with the last star winking out as daylight overshadowed its light.

She had to paint it, see if she could capture the breathtaking array of colors as they reflected off the great gray stone monolithic peaks. On her trek to the stables, the light increased, and the world shook off the night. A hawk issued a piercing screech as it swooped overhead, and had her glancing up to watch as it flew with speed and precision after its next meal. Near the stables, the grumbled low of a cow wafted on the breeze as the animal ambled over the field.

Bianca passed a pair of hikers, their rucksacks bulging with gear stowed on their backs. They turned off onto one of the trail head entrances. Striding past the main hotel, she spied a flurry of activity inside.

Maybe after her riding lesson, she would stop by the restaurant for a proper breakfast.

Bianca arrived at the stables with a minute to spare, and tried to figure out exactly where she was supposed to go. The cowboy hadn't told her where precisely she should meet him. Why would he want to make anything easy for her? The man seemed to get a kick out of antagonizing her to the extreme.

At the front desk, she had a clear view down the main line of walnut wooden stalls. A few horses' heads were poking out over the gates, watching the activity. Probably waiting for the caretakers to feed them. The area was well maintained and clean. The vaulted ceiling made the building appear even larger. And she spied a few hallways that led off from the main row. The scent of hay and manure hung in the air.

Where the hell *was* she supposed to meet the man? If this was a prank, she thought, gritting her teeth, she would make him pay for it.

"You're late," a deep male voice said from behind.

"Bollocks! I am not!" She swiveled around, her heart pounding at the way he had snuck up on her, and glared at the blasted man. "I arrived on time, at a minute to seven. However, you failed to specify precisely where in the stables to meet you."

It was a damn shame that he looked like decadent sin in his cowboy hat and boots. The forest-green plaid shirt already had the cuffs rolled up to near his elbows, giving her ample forearm porn, and stretched over his studly shoulders. Those liquid gold eyes assessed her from head to toe. And heat rushed into her cheeks as she blushed under the intensity of his gaze.

When he didn't make a move or offer a rebuff, she asked, "Shall we get started?"

"This way, princess." He nodded his head toward the open stable door. A man of few words, he strode toward the stall he had indicated, clearly expecting her to follow. His powerful steps had her quickening her pace to keep up with him.

He halted at Sunshine's stall. She was a gorgeous, sweet tempered mare. At their arrival, she poked her tawny head over the door. Her dark eyes filled with recognition of Maverick. She seemed to flirt with the cowboy, nudging him playfully in the chest. And well, who could blame her? The man was sexy as hell no matter what species you were.

He rubbed his big, square hands over Sunshine's nose.

His fingers were long and thick, and the horse looked like she was in heaven at his touch.

And it was insane, but Bianca was jealous... of the damn horse.

"After the lesson, I'll show you where the tack room is and where you will store the gear. For this first lesson, I have everything ready to put the saddle on."

"I know how to put a saddle on a horse." Bianca rubbed a hand over Sunshine's neck, her belly performing somersaults at his nearness, and tried to sound calm.

"I'm sure you do, given your training on the English saddle. However, you don't know Western. There are differences which, while small, are important. If I'm going to teach you, it will be done right. I won't have one of my horses injured over your pride."

Her spine straightened at the implication that he would even insinuate such a thing. "I would never hurt a horse."

"I'm not saying you would intentionally, but maybe through ignorance with the differences in saddles. One of the main distinctions between the two is that the Western is far heavier and bulkier than its English counterpart. I want you to put the saddle pad on Sunshine's back, and then the saddle. This way, I can watch you do it, and assist if needed."

Lifting the latch keeping the gate locked, he slid the wooden stall door over so she could enter. Maverick had his hands on Sunshine, walking her backward.

"Hello sweet girl, remember me?" Bianca followed the rangy cowboy into the stall, withdrew the rest of the apple, and held it out for the sweet mare.

Sunshine snuffled her palm and gently nipped the treat from her hand. Bianca rubbed her nose, getting acquainted with the darling horse. When she felt satisfied that she wouldn't spook the mare, she lifted the saddle blanket from its perch over the stall, inherently aware of Maverick in the small enclosure with her.

How could she not be, when he eclipsed the space? She ignored his intense golden stare as he followed her every move, and talked to Sunshine instead.

"We're going for a bit of a ride this morning. I'm just going to get this blanket on you. Will you let me?"

Sunshine tossed her head up and down in excitement at the prospect of a ride. Thrilled with the horse's inescapable joy, Bianca got a signal to proceed. She tossed the thick blanket over the animal's dappled back then smoothed the material until it lay flat, adjusting it slightly until it was properly settled.

"Now the saddle," he ordered.

Bianca shivered at his deep, rumbling bass. He had one of those masculine voices that tripped every feminine sensor in her, one she was sure was hardwired into women's brains to let them know that they had come across a prime alpha— the type best suited for continuation of the species.

She hated that the sound of his voice sent her pulse thumping, and ravenous need cascading along her spine to pool in her belly.

Ignoring her moronic body and the bloody cowboy, she hoisted the saddle off the wooden stand, shocked by the difference in weight. He hadn't lied about it being heavier. Struggling a bit, she lifted it up over Sunshine's back, and settled it over the saddle pad.

"Good." He helped her cinch the saddle beneath the horse's belly and get all the straps in place. "Now, the bridle and reins are different. Instead of being connected to form one, you have two that are separated. Unlike the English way, you won't need to use as much force with the reins to get Sunshine to proceed in the direction you want her to go. She's been trained to turn left or right with only a light pull in either direction. Let's get you mounted."

He approached, bent down slightly, and laced his hands together for her foot.

"Up with you, now."

As she laid her hands lightly on his shoulders, he pegged her with a deep stare. Everything paused between them; it felt as if time stilled, and the rest of the world faded. Her gaze dropped to his full lips shrouded by dark stubble. Ignoring the desire to discover what his mouth would feel like against hers, she placed her left foot in his joined hands.

But it felt like she was placing so much more than simply her foot there.

Their gazes connected and sizzled. His eyes followed her as she lifted up, grasped the saddle horn, and swung her leg over the saddle. Once she was seated, Maverick adjusted the stirrups, his large hand gripping her ankle until the fit was correct. His touch razored through her, and her flesh continued to burn, even after he released her.

"Now, you want to sit deeply in the saddle with your back straight. Hold the reins in your non-dominant hand; you will not need much force in signaling the direction you want to go with the reins, so keep it light. Give steering signals with your hips. Trail horses have been trained to follow your body signals. The different Western gaits that we will practice in the paddock are: walk, jog, lope, and gallop, which are similar to walk, trot, canter, and gallop in the English style of riding."

She nodded. "Understood."

Maverick led them out of the stall, but then allowed Bianca to steer Sunshine toward the paddock at a nice, ambling walk. Just like with her artwork, she had forgotten how much she adored riding. It was another pastime that had bitten the dust at her mother's insistence.

Maverick opened the paddock door for them. "Take her for a nice walk around the paddock while I close the gate."

With little prodding from Bianca, Sunshine appeared to know the drill and was only too happy to oblige. The slow walk gave Bianca's body a chance to adjust to the saddle. The slightly deeper seat was different than what she was familiar with, but there were enough similarities, all the lessons and skills she had picked up all those years ago returned. It was like her body had the muscle memory.

"Take her up to a jog. You don't need to post, just sit in the saddle and let her do the work. Use your legs to direct her."

Bianca tightened her legs, giving Sunshine the signal to advance. The horse picked up the pace as they rode together around the ring.

Over the next forty-five minutes, Maverick took Bianca through the different signals to get Sunshine to increase her pace, and slow it down. He had her stop and correct her posture a few times. They were minor tweaks Bianca was certain she would nail in no time.

By the time the hour had concluded, there was a huge grin splitting her face. It really was a beautiful morning. Not that she would ever like mornings or be a morning person, but being on horseback again was worth the early wakeup call.

"All right, time to bring her in. Dismount, and lead her inside."

Bianca followed his command. With her feet back on the ground, she gathered Sunshine's reins and headed for the paddock exit.

Maverick held the gate open for them. "You did well. A

few more sessions then, given your riding history, you will be good to go."

"You sound surprised. Did you think I lied about my experience?"

"No, but you forget I don't know you well. You wouldn't be the first tourist to exaggerate your skill level and proficiency." He shrugged and shut the gate once they had cleared it.

"After a few more lessons, I will be able to take Sunshine out for a ride?" She liked the mare, and wanted to explore the area more.

"Not alone, but yes."

"What? Do you think I'm going to run off with her?" She shot him an angry glance.

Maverick pegged her with a glare. "No. But this isn't Buckingham Palace or the genteel English countryside. Out here, you've got mountain lions, black bears, and elk to contend with—in addition to an unfamiliar terrain. It's too dangerous for you to go it alone. Granted, if it was your own horse, we'd let you go off and fend for yourself. But Sunshine is a ranch horse, and we work to make sure our horses are protected from those dangers as much as possible. When you want a trail ride, it will have to be with at least one wrangler from the ranch."

Bianca opened her mouth to argue her point—that she didn't plan to go far, at least not at first, until she was more familiar with the area.

"Those aren't my rules, princess, but ranch policy. If you want to argue your case, take it up with the owner. But I will fight you over it, because while you might be a good rider, you don't know jack about the Rockies or the wilderness."

Bianca realized she would have more luck moving the

mountains than she would getting him to budge from his stance. She understood it, she did, but it still rankled. "Fine. When can I schedule a trail ride? I'd like to do an extended one."

"Do two or three more lessons. Then we can get you set up for a long ride. Once we get Sunshine taken care of and your tack stowed away, we'll put the lessons in the calendar."

More lessons meant more time with him. More snipping and egging one another on. As much as the cowboy drove her batty at times, Bianca enjoyed verbally sparring with him. If she could just manage the undiluted need that hummed in her veins when he was near, it would go a lot smoother for her. She conceded. "Lead the way."

She would ace those lessons if it killed her. Never again would she allow anyone to treat her like she was incompetent while holding her up to higher standards.

7

*T*he following afternoon, Bianca strolled over to the hotel—more specifically, to the restaurant located on the first floor of the lodge, just off to the right of the lobby. As she walked through the spacious entrance, she noted all the decorative touches that created a rustic elegance. She was excited to try the restaurant for the first time, and for the chance to get to know Amber Anderson. They were meeting for a late lunch because of Amber's schedule.

Which ended up being perfect. With the extra time, Bianca had finished setting up her new studio in the spare room.

The delivery had arrived from Archie's Art Supplies at shortly after one yesterday. And Bianca couldn't remember the last time she had enjoyed herself more after the delivery guy left. It was providence she'd had the foresight to purchase a set of rolling drawers in which to store and organize her supplies. She might love art and painting, but she also appreciated order in her life.

If she owned the cabin, there were a few modifications

that she would make. Like building shelves into the walls—some that were expandable—to store her brushes, palettes, pencils, and more.

Bianca had spent the better part of yesterday evening, and again today after her riding lesson, sitting on the front porch with a sketch book. She drew the surrounding fields and mountains from different angles and perspectives. In some, she included her cabin or the hotel or the stables.

Thoughts of the stables brought Maverick to mind. She was doing that a lot lately—thinking about him—and didn't much care for it. She had even done a few sketches of him, of what he looked like leaning against the paddock fence, his gaze intense, or as he was helping her mount Sunshine.

If she didn't know better, she would have said his hands had lingered on her for a few seconds longer than necessary today. And she didn't know if she liked him, or if she was simply growing familiar with his caustic quips.

Shit.

No more thinking about the hot cowboy—er, rather... the stubborn, overbearing cowboy.

Marching toward the hostess stand at the restaurant entrance, she pushed thoughts of him to the back of her mind, instead choosing to focus on the fact that, for the first time in years, the itch to create suffused her. It was bursting through the seams of her control. And if she hadn't needed to leave for lunch with Amber, she would have started on the portrait buzzing her soul.

She promised herself she would dive right in as soon as she returned to the cabin.

When she stepped inside the restaurant, the first thing her senses intercepted was the heady aroma wafting from the kitchen. Her stomach growled, reminding her that she hadn't eaten more than the apple before her ride this morning—she'd been too intent on and lost in getting the sketch she wanted to bring to life in a painting to pause for a snack.

The restaurant was charming with a homespun, family friendly feel. Glancing around the room, she located Amber in a royal blue suit, inky hair spilled in long waves down her back. Amber was sitting catty-cornered to a brunette woman in understated gray trousers and a pale pink blouse.

Relief flowed through Bianca. At least, she wasn't over-dressed for this lunch in her loose-fitting ivory trousers and mint green blouse.

Pasting a friendly smile on her face, she approached the table where the duo were conversing. "Amber."

Amber shot her a smile. "Ah, there you are. I was beginning to wonder if you had forgotten."

Bianca shook her head. "No, I didn't forget, I got caught up. Sorry I'm a few minutes late. It's not like me at all."

"I'm just glad you made it. And I hope you don't mind, but my friend Grace decided to join us," Amber added, and indicated the brunette with kind eyes that were filled with interest.

"No, not at all. It's nice to meet you, Grace." Bianca took a seat in one of the empty chairs.

Leaning forward, Grace said, "Thanks for letting me crash your lunch. I rarely get enough time away from the office for an actual lunch that involves eating. When Amber mentioned she was having a girls' lunch with another city slicker, I sort of invited myself."

Bianca chuckled as her anxiety diminished. "You're from the city as well, but live here now?" The idea of it wriggled into her brain.

"Yes; I lived in Denver for many years. If it weren't for meeting my husband and inheriting my grandpa's practice, I would still be living there. But once I met Emmett, my life in the big city ended." Grace beamed a bit, talking about her hubby.

Amber added, "Grace is the town doctor. One of them, anyway. We do have a medical center in Winter Park as well, but if you need medical care, she's the best."

Grace put her hands to her chest and said to Amber, "Aw, I appreciate that." Then she said to Bianca, "My practice is in town, should you have any medical needs or issues crop up."

"That's good to know, and I will keep that in mind if the need arises. So your husband works for the ranch?" Bianca asked Grace, interested because the woman seemed so polished.

"Yes, he's one of the wranglers. We live in a cabin on ranch property," Grace explained.

"It must be lovely. And Amber, you own the ranch?" Bianca asked her, rather fascinated by both women. They were giving her ideas—ones she was terrified of. If these urban, forward-thinking women could live here and thrive, why couldn't she?

Amber ignored the call buzzing on her phone, and silenced it before replying. "Yeah, my family owns the ranch. I have only been in charge of general operations of Silver Springs Ranch since last fall. Prior to that, it was my older brother, Colt, who held the position."

"Amber, would you and your guests like to order?" They were interrupted by the waitress, who was a few years older, with touches of silver strands in her hair, adorned in what looked like the requisite uniform of black trousers and a white, long-sleeved shirt.

"Jean, just give us a few minutes. We got caught up

gabbing and didn't look at the menus." Amber smiled at the waitress.

"If you two know what you want, give her your orders, and by the time you're done, I should know what I want," Bianca stated, flipping the menu open.

Amber studied her with a raised brow, then nodded and turned to her friend. "All right. Grace, you're up."

"You know me, Jean, I want the brisket sandwich with... oh to hell with it, give me the fries, and an iced tea with lemon."

"Got it. And for you, boss?"

Amber glared at Grace in mock outrage. "You just had to go and order that, didn't you? Damn, I'll do an extra fifteen on the elliptical tomorrow. I'll have what Grace is having."

All three women turned their gazes in Bianca's direction. "Well, if the sandwich is that nommy, I'll give it a go," she said. "Make that three."

"Yes! See, I knew you were a woman after my own heart." Amber grinned and did a little wiggle in her seat.

"And we need more of us. We're so outnumbered by the male population in this area," Grace stated, and leaned forward conspiratorially. "There are even days when I long for traffic. How sad is that!"

"Really?" Bianca asked, and barked out a laugh.

"Yes." Grace nodded emphatically.

"You were telling me about your brother, Amber. Did something happen to him?" Bianca nudged the conversation back in that direction.

"Oh, right. Yeah, but nothing like what you're assuming. Last fall, Colt met Avery. She was staying in one of the out of the way cabins on the property. The moment they met, it was pretty much all they wrote for those two. Totally neck deep in love. They were married in February, on the beach. It was a beautiful ceremony. Now my brother travels around the world with her. She's this big shot scientist, currently working with NASA, discovering comets and asteroids. Probably going to win a Nobel Prize at some point in her life. But to be with Avery, Colt handed the operations over to me," Amber explained.

"He gave up his career for his wife?" Bianca asked, rather amazed that a man would do that sort of thing. In her world, in the future that was planned, Peter would be aghast if she asked him to be the one keeping house and home in line, chairing committees, and charities, while she went and worked in the House of Lords.

"Yeah, isn't it sweet? Emmett was willing to give up his life here to move to Denver with me. That's how I knew he was a keeper. Well, that, and the man is stunning naked." Grace sighed.

"I've almost forgotten what a naked man looks like, it's been so long since I've gotten any." Amber frowned.

"Well, your problem is that you are hung up on one man. If you looked further afield..." Grace drifted off as their meal was delivered.

Once it was just the three of them again, Amber cocked her head. "So, Bianca—"

"Yes?" Anxiety filled her as both women looked expectantly at her.

"Do you have any guys waiting on you back in London?" Amber asked.

"Yes, we want to know what it's like. I mean, you've got all those guys with those gorgeous accents." Grace sighed.

Amber took a bite of a fry with her head tilted as they waited for Bianca's reply. There was no way she could answer the question without getting bogged down in details.

And to be honest, she didn't consider herself involved with Peter. It was more that they were fellow hostages attempting to appease their jailors.

So Bianca lied. "No, not at the moment. My life has become something unrecognizable. One I don't particularly care for, which is why I'm here."

"Someone told me my wife was here. I didn't believe them. I thought surely, if my wife was close by, she would have stopped at the stables to see me. Yet, I find her here. I'm wounded," a deep male voice teased as a rather gorgeous, tall cowboy appeared at Grace's side, smiling down at her with such devotion in his gaze, Bianca wondered if they should give the couple some privacy.

"Hi honey, I was going to stop by on my way back to the office." Grace smiled sheepishly up at him, trying not to laugh.

"Uh huh." He gave her some side eye brimming with carnal heat that had Grace squirming in her seat.

"Emmett, have you met Bianca? She's staying at the ranch for the next few weeks. She's visiting us from London." Grace gestured across the table.

Emmett turned his frosted blue gaze in Bianca's direction and gave her a lopsided grin. "It's a pleasure, Bianca. I saw you this morning with Maverick in the paddock. You looked like you belong in that saddle."

Pleased at the compliment and thinking that Grace was a lucky woman indeed, Bianca explained, "He's helping me switch saddle styles. I learned to ride on the English saddle, did dressage, jumping, and the like for years. I'm hoping to do some of the longer trail rides and maybe even one of the cattle drives once I'm well versed enough on the Western saddle."

"That's why you look like you were bred to it. Welcome

—get yourself signed up, and I'll put you to work rounding up cattle." He winked. Then he shifted his attention back to Grace, cupped her nape, and kissed her.

Christ! By the time Emmett had finished kissing Grace, the woman was simpering and starry eyed. And Bianca wanted to fan her face at the nuclear level heat pumping off those two.

"See you at home, love." Emmett flashed a seductive grin, and headed off.

Grace sighed as he walked away. "You could bounce a nickel off it."

Bianca and Amber turned their heads and watched Grace's husband retreat. Bianca had to admit, the man did have a great set of buns. "Probably more like a quarter for a back end that fine."

Amber snorted. "His buns aren't bad..."

Grace chuckled. "Bianca, I knew I liked you. And Amber, his are only not bad because there's another guy's derriere you want to grab."

"And who is that? Does he work here?" Bianca asked, as she thought of Maverick and the way he wore a pair of jeans. And while Emmett sported a good backside, the sight of Maverick's tight end and the way his jeans fit him made naughty fantasies of clutching his ass as he drove inside her fill her mind. She shoved those thoughts away, lest she do something moronic, like act on them.

Grace leaned forward and whispered conspiratorially, "She's got the hots for Lincoln. Not that I blame her, because the man is sexy as hell."

More relieved than she cared to admit that it wasn't Maverick, Bianca lowered her voice and said, "I don't think I've met him yet. What does he look like?"

With a frustrated sigh, Amber said, "He's Mister Tall,

Dark, and Grumpy, like a giant tree I want to climb and do all manner of wicked deeds with."

Bianca bit her bottom lip, trying to contain her mirth, but after one look at Grace attempting to muffle her laughter, she lost it. They all cackled, sounding like a pack of hyenas, and drew stares from other restaurant patrons.

All in all, it was the most fun Bianca had had at a lunch in years—if not ever. Warmth filled her chest, because for the first time in a long time—since the four semesters she had studied in Italy—she was being accepted not because of her family or her station, but because of who she was, and it was an incredible, addictive sensation.

When she finally exited the restaurant, the idea for her upcoming painting blazed in her soul. And with it, there was a spring in her step, and a lightness in her heart.

8

*M*averick propped himself back against the wooden fence, his arms crossed in front of his chest, studying the rider atop Sunshine. He couldn't fault her ability, or how well she had adjusted to riding Western. Bianca and Sunshine had bonded over the past few days. Each morning, Bianca brought Sunshine an apple or carrot, and had earned the mare's undying adoration in the process.

Regal was the word that came to mind when Bianca rode. She looked like a queen, getting ready to inspect her troops. And Sunshine responded to her rider's pose, like she knew Bianca was a cut above the rest of them, matching her in grace and form.

As someone who was raised riding horses, had been around them his entire life, Mav rarely stopped to admire the way a person rode. But Bianca was magnificent. She rode as well as he and the rest of the wranglers—possibly even better, given her attention to form. Not that he would ever admit that to her. And he hadn't been the only one who had noticed—Emmett and Tanner had both made comments.

But he didn't want to share her. He wasn't certain where this possessiveness he felt toward her came from, except that it was there.

He didn't like her.

Yet, she had grown on him, his esteem for her rising day by day with her lessons. And there wasn't really any reason for them to continue other than it would give him an excuse to watch her.

It meant they were no longer going to be in each other's hair. Unless he led a trail ride that she signed up for in the next few weeks, they wouldn't be seeing each other. Granted, he could always lie and have her continue the lessons.

In truth, if he didn't have a pile of work staring him in the face, he would stay and observe her riding. The woman was sexy as hell, even when she glared down her nose at him. It made the sadist in him want to rile her up just to get a reaction. If he didn't know better, he would say he looked forward to bickering with her each day. And the way her stellar cleavage bounced as horse and rider galloped around the ring sent his thoughts veering into dangerous territory—imagining what her tits would look like above him as she rode him.

He'd been fighting a hard-on since the moment she arrived at the stables.

"Ease her down to a lope." He shouted the command.

Bianca gave him a curt nod. He monitored the way her knees and body moved as she slowed Sunshine's gait.

Checking the time, he grimaced and called out, "All right, bring her in. That's all the time we have for today."

Bianca slowed Sunshine's pace more, and they slowly

plodded his way. When they reached his side, he had already moved away from the fence. He gripped the reins to steady Sunshine while her rider dismounted. "Come on down. I think you're ready for a trail ride."

"Finally! It's about bloody time," Bianca exclaimed. She took her feet out of the stirrups, leaned forward, and swung her right leg over Sunshine's back to dismount.

But she had overcompensated with the force, and gasped as she lost her grip on the saddle horn. Before she could tumble to the ground, Mav caught her around the waist, shifting her into his arms.

"Bollocks," she hissed, twisting her upper torso and grabbing his shoulders.

He shifted her body in his hands; the move brought her figure into full contact with his body. Maverick stared, his gaze fixed on her face, as he lowered her down slowly, one inch at a time. Her body slid against him, leaving a trail of fire in its wake. Stirred, he gripped her tighter, then one of his hands lowered and cupped her bottom. He squeezed the globe as she descended, her gaze wide.

A wildfire burned through them.

The pulse in her neck fluttered wildly. She wet her lips as she stared at his mouth, and it made his groin tighten. And her pupils dilated as desire took over.

She felt phenomenal pressed against him. Her body was soft in all the right places. When her feet touched the ground, her hands still clung to his shoulders. Her nails dug into his flesh.

Christ, he yearned to suck on the rapid pulse point. Nip her plush bottom lip between his teeth, and work his way down with his mouth to those plump globes.

Her gaze was fixed on his lips, her breathing erratic, and her skin flushed.

Fuck. She wanted him.

And to be honest, all the razzing and needling had been a way of deflecting his interest, given their caustic back and forth. Because he wanted her with a fierceness he didn't quite understand. He physically ached to taste her. Wondered if she remained an impervious ice queen during sex, or if the right partner could strip away all the pretenses and find the passionate woman underneath.

His hands slid up her supple back, his intent clear as day.

She swallowed, her breath sped up, and she licked her bottom lip again. But she wasn't pushing him away. Instead, her fingers curled into his chest like she wanted to hold on.

He swore beneath his breath.

As he lowered his head, everything inside him tightened. His blood pumped fast and furiously. And he hungered—for her.

"Ah, Maverick. We have an issue..."

The sound of Trevor's voice broke them apart—or, more aptly, she jumped back out of Mav's arms. Embarrassment flashed over her face. Her chest rose and fell with her breathing. Mav kept his gaze on Bianca as he spoke to Trevor. "What's the problem?"

"Dolly threw a shoe and is limping on that leg a bit," Trevor explained.

Fuck.

"All right, I'm on my way. Let's get Sunshine back in her stall," Mav instructed Bianca.

"I can take care of her while you see to the other horse. I know how to care for them. I'll get her brushed down, tack stowed, and everything. You can double check the work I did after you've finished with Dolly," she offered, taking Sunshine's reins.

"Fine. Much appreciated." He nodded and opened the paddock gate.

Sunshine and Bianca plodded past him, not stopping to wait for him, and walked into the stables. Mav stared for a moment, getting the lust raging through his system under control, before he headed in with Trevor.

And he wondered what would have happened if they hadn't been interrupted. The princess was likely far too vanilla for his darker tastes. He could picture her running away, screaming at the top of her lungs, the moment he broke out the handcuffs and butt plug.

———

"GENTLEMEN. If we could all take our seats, we have a lot of ground to cover today and just a short time to do it in." Amber worked to bring the conference room to order later that day for their department head meeting.

Maverick liked Amber. He had no problem with the job she was doing running the place. Although he did miss his buddy Colt, he had never seen the man happier than he was with Avery.

Mav leaned back in his seat, and glanced at the people in the room.

Noah and Duncan stopped their argument the moment Amber corrected them, and slid into their chairs. Noah removed his Stetson and rested it on the table. His bronze hair stuck up in spikes, like he couldn't be bothered to tame it. As a widower and single father to twin boys, he tended to always be running. Duncan no longer kept his black hair military short like he had in the Navy, and was sporting a beard left over from winter.

Lincoln was already in his seat. He glared at Amber

with an obvious chip on his shoulder, and there was a tic in his jaw. Mav had no idea what was up with them, other than that he would rather drop into a nest full of cotton-mouths than get between those two.

At least the meeting this afternoon was only for department heads and not a full staff meeting. Those tended to get much livelier.

"Noah, what's the status on the herd? Anything we need to do as we head into our busy season?" Amber asked with a pen in her hand poised over a legal pad.

"Actually, we're busy enough that I think we should expand the herd. We have enough in the budget, and the space to add an additional twenty. There's an auction coming up at the end of May on the outskirts of Denver which I think we should attend," Noah said, and handed her a thick file.

"We can add that to our schedule. Are you sure we need that many?" Amber asked, glancing through the information.

Noah rolled his shoulders and said, "Yes, I do. We have some of our older stock coming up on retirement by the end of this year. I have listed the horses that will be heading to our retirement stables and farm. If we bring in another twenty this summer, we won't overload the older horses, and can begin to prep for the turnover in the fall. And we should consider adding another twenty next year as well. I've got all the numbers on that for you."

"I agree with you. Are we experiencing enough growth with the demand for trail rides that we need to build more stables and really increase the herd?" Amber cocked her head.

Noah shook his head. "No, I don't think so, not yet. Mav, what do you think? Do we need additional stables?"

"We aren't there yet, Amber. And I would tell you if we were. But I do agree with Noah that some of our elderly stock need to be given some freedom from having to work in their remaining twilight years. With our current slate of seasonal and year round staff, we can handle the additional twenty or so horses with no problems," Mav said.

"Okay, good to know. Noah, where are we with vaccinations and the like?" Amber asked.

Noah replied, "Right on schedule. I've got my team checking hooves, reshoeing all the ones that are worn, loose, or otherwise. By the time our summer season begins, our horses will be ready for the deluge of tourists and in tip top shape."

"Good, well done. Lincoln, what's the status on the repairs to the cabins that were damaged in those hail storms?" Amber shifted her gaze to the opposite side of the table and zeroed in on Lincoln.

"They're coming along at a nice clip. However, I think, given that we're already working to make repairs, we should implement our plans to move the cabins off grid and install the solar panels to power them," Lincoln explained with a nonchalant shrug.

"You think that could be completed before high season begins next month?" she asked.

Lincoln rubbed at the back of his neck before he responded. "Adding that work order to each cabin's manifest of repairs will extend the repair time. There's no way around that. I've outlined the extra time in my report. As long as the weather holds, I project we should be able to get all but five cabins fully repaired by month's end. The rest I can finish up during the first part of June, while my team is on hand for maintenance with the flood of visitors. But, keep in mind, while my crew and I work hard, I can't guarantee Mother Nature isn't going to get pissed, drop two feet of snow on us that takes a week to melt, and toss a wrench in my timetable."

"We're all governed by that finicky bitch. Before I give you the go ahead, I want to check our bookings for June, and see if we can manage without those five cabins before I give you the green light," Amber said. "Give me twenty-four hours to look over those numbers and I will get back to you on that. Duncan, what do you have for me?"

Duncan said, "Well, like I thought, the desire for survival training has picked up in recent months. I know we talked about having day camps for kids this summer. I think it will be manageable, but I will need help because I can't be everywhere at once. So the week or two in which we schedule the camp, I wouldn't be able to do overnight survival training."

"What if we have it for one week in June, and then again in July for one week? That way, we could just mark on the website that the overnight training we offer isn't available during those weeks. And we do have it in the budget to hire some help seasonally if you wanted it," Amber offered.

"Two of my buddies I served with are looking for work. They both just retired from the Navy. I'd like to bring them on, possibly for longer than just seasonal work," Duncan explained.

"Get me their resumes and I'll take a look. If they have other skillsets that we can rotate them to handle, a more permanent position might be feasible. Would they be able to do overnight survival training in the weeks you'd be unavailable due to the camps?" Amber asked, looking like she was calculating expenses in her head.

"Absolutely. If we can get them here in the next week or

so, I could have them go on a few overnights with me so that they would know the drill. I'll call them and have them email you right away." Duncan nodded.

"Good, I like the sound of that." Amber's gaze, so like her brother's, landed on Maverick. "Mav, how's the wrangling looking for this summer?"

"Most of our seasonal guides have signed on again. If Duncan's friends are any good with horses and cattle, I could use the added help. He and I could work out their schedules to make it work."

Amber nodded. "I will take that into consideration. Can your friends ride, Duncan?"

"They're good enough, and will get better with experience," Duncan said.

"That would work for me. Anything else?" Amber asked, glancing around the room.

"Actually, there is something Noah and I have been discussing, going back and forth over—especially once you started talking about survival training day camps for kids. We've debated the possibility of hosting horse riding day camps. We'd likely want to keep the age brackets to middle school and high school to start with, see if there's an interest. Construct the camp so they don't just learn to ride, but how to care for a horse, muck out the stall, those types of things. With the last day culminating with a three-hour trail ride with lunch," Maverick explained, and shot Noah a glance. It had come about through a discussion about Noah's boys and teaching them about horses. His twins were four, little hellions who kept making nannies quit, but when it came time for them to be with the horses, they settled down and followed directions.

"That sounds interesting. We've not announced the day camp for the survival training, but maybe we could have two different sessions in between those two. Have you worked up the numbers on that?" Amber asked.

"We have. It's here in the report." He handed it over.

"All right. I will examine what you've put together, see if it's something we can budget for this summer. If not, it's certainly an idea I really like that, looking ahead, we may be able to add next year," Amber said, checking her watch. "If that's all you have for me, I can let you guys get back to work."

They all looked at each other, waiting for someone to speak.

"Great. Then we can reconvene in two weeks. I'll email you guys the time. Great work everyone," she said, and gave them a big smile.

They rose from their seats. Lincoln was out the door in a flash. Mav really needed to ask him what the hell was up between him and the boss. Noah and Duncan trailed behind Lincoln, until it was just Mav and Amber left in the conference room.

Before he could depart, Amber said, "Mav, hold up a minute."

"What's up?" Mav knew there were some on the ranch who didn't love the fact that Amber was in charge now. But he couldn't fault her. She worked hard, had ventured down some paths that her brother had resisted, and had achieved great results.

"Our guest from London, Bianca Peabody?" she said with a frank stare.

He bit back a curse. The confounded British woman needed a good spanking. Had she complained about him?

She was the type to do it. And if she had complained, had she also mentioned this morning, when they had come close to locking lips?

He clenched his fists as he saw red. It didn't matter that before her riding lessons, she snuck Sunshine apples and had the mare eating out of her hand. Or that she looked sexy as hell on horseback with a skill that few could muster.

"What about her?" he asked, unable to keep the derisive tone out of his voice.

"I'd just like you to be nice to her."

"I am nice, but she can be rather difficult. I realize she's a guest, and I will do what I can to lay off a bit." The damn woman made him want to swear off the species and become a monk.

"I think she's lonely, is what she is, and a little lost," Amber said with a shrug.

Mav ignored the hole that punched through his chest. He didn't want to feel bad for the woman. Hell, he didn't want to feel anything for her, and that included the ever-present lust that powered through him any time she was near. "Then you be nice to her. I'm not here to cater to that princess's every whim."

Amber frowned and crossed her arms. "No. But you are paid to cater to mine. And I'm telling you now, stop being a jerk. I know you can charm the ladies, Mav. Give her some of the charm and have her eating out of your hand. She's spending a lot of money with us for the foreseeable future, and I would rather not have her decide to cut her stay short because someone's nose was out of joint. Understood?"

"Perfectly," he replied, imagining taking that woman over his knee.

"Good. Cause I think the money we're making off her stay will go a long way toward paying for that day camp idea."

That was a sneaky tactic on Amber's part, and she knew

it. He seethed. "Can I ask, did the princess complain about me?"

"Nope. I noticed it the other day as she was leaving one of your riding lessons. I watched your interaction and the way you talked to her. If it had been me, I would have cleaned your clock. But then again, I was raised around cowboys like you all my life, and don't scare easy. Something tells me that Miss Peabody has led a rather sheltered life, and doesn't quite know how to take you. So lay off being an asshole, or I will bloody your lip for her."

He had considered that too about Bianca, but figured he was simply being fanciful because of what she did to his internal combustion. But if Amber saw the same thing? Then shit, he was being a dick. It didn't matter that he got a sadistic thrill out of sparring with her. Not if it truly caused her pain. They weren't going to be seeing each other every day, and less interaction between them would help.

"I'll see what I can do, but I won't make any promises. And it was your brother who taught you how to protect yourself and take someone down. Well, who the hell do you think taught him?"

Maverick strode out of the conference room. The princess hadn't complained about him, and that was something, at least.

Damn woman. He rubbed a hand over his stomach at the thought of her, at the need clawing at him to be set free. The last thing he needed to do was consider what the princess looked like naked.

9

On Saturday evening, Bianca stood before the canvas that was bursting with vibrant life—one she had created—and rejoiced. She hadn't lost her abilities. If anything, her skill with the brush was better than she remembered, like she had been waiting for the right push and place to truly begin.

Her phone rang. She didn't look at the name before answering. She was too full of herself and the glorious image on her easel. Elation swam through her. Joy spilled out of every pore.

"Hello."

"When are you coming home? You are being reckless and foolish. Peter is worried sick about you." Her mother's voice blasted through the phone.

Oh really? If he was so worried, then why hadn't he called her at all this past week?

Only one week.

That was all the freedom she had garnered from her mother. It was Bianca's fault. She should have checked the caller's name on her phone screen before answering, and sent it to voicemail like all the others. All the elation and pride that had infused her moments prior took a nosedive. Well, her day had gone all to pot rather quickly.

"I can't talk to you right now, Mother. I am busy."

"That's rubbish. Now listen to me, missy, you will collect your things and head home immediately."

"No. I can't do that." Even the thought of it made the spurting flame inside her, the one that moments before had glistened at wattages to compete with the sun, dim.

"Nonsense. You can, and you will. Stop being difficult. This is so typical of you."

"I'm sorry you see it that way, but I'm not coming back yet."

"Well, when can we expect you back?" she sniped.

Never. If Bianca had her way, then she would never return. "I'm not sure. I will let you know."

"Now listen here and listen good, if you think to back out of your commitments and embarrass your father and me, the consequences will be severe."

"I'm not doing this to hurt you or anyone." It was just that Bianca was drowning, and no one from her life had even noticed. Not a single person saw that she was merely going through the motions and couldn't even see herself any more.

"Of course you are. This is the thanks I always get."

"I've got to go, Mother. We'll talk later." Bianca hung up without even giving her mum a chance to say goodbye.

Her mother would just go on and on for infinity. And Bianca would cave then, like she always did, to make her stop.

She swiped at the stray tear. Not once had she ever measured up to her mother's impossible standards. Bianca had tried for her entire life, putting aside what she wanted, and yielding to her mother's tedious demands.

But recently, she had come to the realization that no matter how hard she tried, she never would measure up. Her mother would always find fault with her, be it her looks, actions, or words. She was either too loud or didn't speak up enough. She wasn't thin enough or she was too thin. When it came to the ample size of her cleavage, she was told she really should get something done about it, and her mother had just the doctor Bianca should see to take care of the problem... and on and on.

Bianca was exhausted from her failed attempts. She couldn't continue living a life she hated—not just hated, but loathed with every fiber of her being. She had plenty of friends, but not a single one she was truly close to. She didn't even know if her friends liked her for herself, or because of who she was and the position she held in polite society.

None of them had called to check up on her, not even her bridesmaids or maid of honor.

She removed her smock, not caring that there were a few smudges of paint that had made it past the apron onto her oversized button-down shirt and black leggings. Leaving the sanctuary of her pseudo art studio, needing fresh air after the talk with her mum, she headed for the porch outside. On her way out the door, her mobile rang again. It was her mother calling back. She tossed the bloody thing on the couch and kept on walking.

No more answering the phone until she knew who was calling.

Barefoot, the wood smooth beneath her feet, she made it across the porch and descended two steps down. As the fight leeched out of her, she lowered herself and plopped her butt on the top step, swimming in such misery, not even the spectacular color palette the setting sun had turned the sky could shake her out of her malaise.

Bianca lowered her head into her hands, with her elbows resting on her thighs. It was exhausting talking to her mother. She hadn't realized just how much a conversation drained her until she'd escaped this past week.

"Everything all right, princess?"

It bloody well figured. Like her day hadn't descended into the eleventh circle of hell already. What was one more trial? Would the man mock her supreme embarrassment just to cap off a perfectly wretched day?

"Go away," she mumbled, not bothering to lift her head. She didn't have the energy to deal with Maverick—or anyone, really. But the blasted cowboy was the last person she wanted to be around.

When his dark brown boots entered her line of sight, she sighed. Why wasn't the man going away? With a snarky retort on her tongue, she finally lifted her face. But she was struck again by the hard angles of his rough-hewn jaw covered with dark stubble, by the sharp blades of his cheekbones, adding strength and resolve to his features, and at the firm slashes of his thick, dark brows, shrouding eyes that, in the descending sunset, looked like pools of liquid gold.

Testosterone belched off him; he was encased in a ruggedness that tripped all the angry wires inside her. Every time she was near him, those stupid wires got their signals crossed and her body hummed with potent arousal, much like an electrical grid powering up.

"Not until you tell me what's wrong," he stated firmly, studying her with an impassive expression she was too tired to decipher.

"Why are you even being nice to me?" She couldn't

handle anyone being fake around her any longer. It was
what the entire ghastly scope of her life had been, and she
was done with it, for as long as she could manage. She didn't
even know who *she* was anymore. Only that she was an
engaged woman not in love with the groom, who detested
her life, who had boarded a plane and traveled five thousand miles to escape it all.

And in one week, she was happier here than she had
been in the past year.

He shrugged those wide, muscled shoulders in a
nonchalant manner, stretching the confines of his navy
plaid shirt. "You looked like you could use a friend. Figured
I'd lend a hand if I could."

"How about a drink?" The offer left her lips before the
words connected with her brain.

Bollocks! What the bloody hell was she thinking?

Mortified that she had made the offer, she ignored the
temptation to peep at his face because she didn't want to
find horror in his expression at the invitation. She was ready
to play it cool and act like it had never happened.

"I could join you for a drink," he replied, and held out a
hand to help her to her feet.

She kept her mouth from dropping open at his response,
but just barely. She nodded, unsure what to do with the big
cowboy, and rose from her seat without taking his hand.
Every time she touched him during riding lessons, sparks
flared in her body. It was the last thing she wanted to feel
when her life was in such disarray.

"I don't have any beer," she said in a last-ditch effort to
avoid having him in her cabin.

"Wine works, in a pinch."

The blasted man was being far too reasonable. And
nice. It set her teeth on edge.

"Actually, I could use some scotch," she said. His eyes widened in disbelief. Those thick brows disappeared beneath his cowboy hat.

At this point, she could use the entire bottle of scotch. She had earned it.

Bianca headed inside. If Maverick followed her, he did. If not, that was fine too.

Behind her, the firm clomp of his boots against the hardwood floor trailed her. He'd chosen door number two. Bianca went directly into the kitchen and headed to the cabinet where she was storing alcohol for the duration of her stay. Eyeing the cabinet interior, she thought she should probably be concerned about the sheer volume of wine and spirits tucked inside. But at the moment, she couldn't care less.

Actually, what she should do was toast her foresight to have it all on hand.

She withdrew the unopened bottle of *Glenlivet 25 Year* scotch, choosing that brand instead of the *Macallan Edition Number Two* which, while a stellar whiskey, she reserved for special occasions. From another cabinet, she removed two clear glass tumblers. They weren't the Waterfords her father preferred but they would do.

Bianca shot Maverick a glance over her shoulder. He stood there, power and testosterone pumping off him, leaning back against the kitchen island. "On the rocks, or straight up?" she asked. She liked it on the rocks herself, and withdrew an ice tray from the freezer.

"Straight up is fine." He was pensive, analyzing her. And not for the first time, she wondered what he saw when he looked at her.

Did he see that she felt like she was suffocating in her own life? That she was running away from everyone and everything she had ever known, and didn't want to go back? Did he see that she was terrified that somehow, some way, she would be dragged back to that life, and end up being one of those empty shell people others looked at and couldn't help but think: what the hell happened to them?

With those thoughts swirling in her mind, she poured three fingers for each of them and handed him a glass.

Maverick toasted her and then took a sip. Sheer delight and appreciation filled his visage. "Now that's some fine scotch. What is that?"

"The *Glenlivet 25*. I can always open the *Macallan Edition* if you would prefer that." She cursed internally. Always the people pleaser, Bianca. Could take the girl out of her polite society but couldn't seem to shake her manners.

His brows rose at her response. "This is fine. Some of the best I've tasted."

She studied him over the rim of her glass as he stared back, then took a sip of the scotch and let the smooth flavor roll around on her tongue as a reckless idea surged to the forefront of her mind. But as the notion surfaced, her entire being lit up and made her feel alive—just as alive as painting had done for her the last few days.

She swallowed the potent drink, the slick burn sliding down her throat into her belly, and said, "I think we should have sex."

He choked on a sip of whiskey, pounded on his chest, cleared his throat, and said, "Excuse me?"

"I said, I think we should have sex. We're both rather forthright individuals, are we not? You're a rather strapping guy, and I figure we're always sniping at one another. It would likely make for some interesting bed sport."

Maverick stared at her like she suddenly had grown snakes for hair that fanned around her face, Medusa style.

But did the man do anything or answer her? Nope. That was new for her: stunning a man silent.

"Oh, did I cross some cultural line? Are women not as open about sex in America?" She tried to play it off like she wasn't absolutely mortified.

"No, you surprised me, and I'm not easily shocked. I doubt it would be a good idea, you and me."

"That's rubbish. Does your cock not work properly? Or am I that unattractive? Oh god, you've got some little tart at home, is that it?" She put a hand against her chest because in truth, when the idea had struck her, she hadn't even considered that he could have a significant other at home. *Pot, meet kettle.*

With a guarded expression, he shook his head. "No. But I like sex on the rough side, and doubt someone with your... sensibilities would be able to handle it."

Oh, was that all? He liked it rough? Good, she didn't want romantic promises and feats of love. She wanted dark and dirty, balls to the wall, sex. She wanted to stop thinking about all the ways she had failed in her life and do something thoroughly irresponsible, like have a tawdry one-night stand with a man she didn't particularly like but who stirred her body.

She knocked back the last finger of scotch like it was water. Maverick cocked a dark brow. Bianca approached him slowly. Put a little sway into her step. Unbuttoning her oversized paint shirt on her trek, she kept her gaze locked on his until she stood six inches from him, and let the material slip off her shoulders. He smelled of horse and leather and distinctly, utterly male. The combination was intoxicating.

She had fantastic breasts, she was aware of that. Men

tended to look at them and not her. And the simple, white lace demi bra she was wearing beneath her top made her double Ds look fabulous.

"Look, princess, I don't think this is a good idea," he said. But that tawny, golden gaze slid down and stared greedily at her chest.

"Why?" *Got him!*

"Because I don't."

Bullshit!

She stepped close to his rock-hard body, and stared into his eyes. "I've been making all the right decisions throughout my life and have hated every blasted second of it. You might be a bad decision, but fuck it, I'm down for making some bad decisions. I don't need gentle, or promises of tomorrow. Take me to bed, Maverick."

She leaned up, keeping her eyes open and on him. Then she leaned in and brushed her lips against his firm mouth. His body was rigid and unmoving.

When he didn't respond to her advances, Bianca lowered back down onto her heels and stepped back. What the hell? She had tried. What was one more embarrassment to add to her tally? Time for more alcohol, and shooing the cowboy out of the cabin. She swiveled away from him with every intention of drowning herself in scotch tonight.

Maverick gripped her arm and spun her around until she was plastered against his hotrod body. Big, calloused hands cupped her nape, tilted her mouth up, and then his mouth crushed her lips. His lips moved with firm intent, and told her in two seconds that he was the one in charge.

Oh, fuck!

She was utterly gobsmacked by the centrifugal force of desire spinning her head. His kiss was greedy and dominant. It was everything she had been missing in her life—

passionate and wicked—as his tongue sought entrance. Caught up in his possession, she opened to him.

Bianca had been kissed before. But until Maverick placed his lips upon hers, she had never experienced this dissolution of everything she was as he molded her and took. He demanded her participation with each sinful thrust of his tongue. His voracious mouth stoked the flames of passion inside her to blistering heights. And she worried that she would spontaneously combust from the intensity of her desire.

She fisted her hands in his hair, knocking off his hat. But she didn't want him to stop—was afraid it would be over before it had really begun, and she discovered she was famished.

Bianca had believed she had known what hunger, desire, and passion were, but as his mouth moved with wicked abandon, the deft sure strokes of his tongue plunging deep and tangling with hers, her assumption was corrected. Every kiss she had experienced prior to Maverick's had been mere imitations.

This was passion in all its untold glory. She moaned into his mouth, gripping him tighter, and kissed him back with all the pent-up need filling her soul from a lifetime spent hiding it.

He changed the angle, backed her up against the counter, and turned the lip lock into the most carnal kiss of her life.

Bianca shook with need. Flames licked against her skin. His hands caressed down her back and cupped her bottom, bringing her against the hard ridge of his desire.

God, this was what she needed more than anything else. She lifted a leg up, needing to get closer, and wrapped it around his waist.

He groaned and ripped his mouth away. Those golden pools of his eyes had darkened with desire. "Be sure, princess," he said, breathing heavily.

"Maverick, take me to bed and fuck my brains out."

On a rough, male groan, he muttered, "Don't forget I warned you."

Then his mouth crashed down over hers. Victory flooded through her as he lifted her other leg up, wrapping it around his waist. With his mouth on hers, he carried her back to the bedroom.

As far as bad decisions went, this was the best one she had made in years.

10

*M*averick kicked the bedroom door closed behind them. The act winnowed everything down to just the two of them, shutting the rest of the world out completely. Colors from the setting sun blazed through the wooden-slatted blinds, blanketing the room in an array of golds and oranges.

He laid Bianca on the bed and tore his mouth away. His thumbs hooked around the waistband of her leggings and slid the material down her legs.

As she lay before him in her bra and panties, quivering with need, his hungry gaze caressed her from head to toe and everywhere in between. She panted, and her nipples grew taut beneath the lacy fabric as she waited in delicious anticipation for what he would do next.

Propping his hands on either side of her shoulders, he wedged his hips between her thighs and leaned down. "Keep your hands at your sides. Don't move them unless I tell you to. Understood?"

She nodded as her mouth went dry and she whispered, "Yes."

He flashed her a potent, sexy smirk, shifted even closer, and drew the bra straps down her arms—with his teeth.

Bianca shuddered. She was in way over her head with him. But she was also far past the point of being able to stop.

Once her shoulders were bared, Maverick trailed hot kisses over them that scorched her from the point of contact and blasted through the rest of her body. She fought to keep her hands at her sides, wishing she could touch him now that she was committed to this path. His hands slid beneath her back, making her arch as he unlatched her bra clasp.

There was no fumbling on his part. Those work-roughened fingers glided over her skin and peeled her bra off. The moment they were free of the material, her breasts spilled out.

"Jesus Christ," he groaned roughly.

And then his hot mouth closed around an areola, tugging the bud deep into his mouth. Her eyes crossed. Her hands dug into the mattress. She arched her back, feeding him the mound. Pleasure swirled and tumbled through her as he sucked the nipple. His hand kneaded its twin, plucking and rolling the nipple between the rough pads of his fingers.

He switched his mouth to the other breast, lashing his tongue over the peak.

The fact that he was still fully clothed while she was wearing nothing but an ivory slip of lace over her bare mound wasn't lost on her. There was something so damn erotic about it.

She wanted to hurry him up, make him bypass foreplay and get to the good part. "Maverick, I need your clothes off and you in me."

He lifted his mouth from her boob with a popping sound.

"Let's get one thing straight: I'm in charge, princess. You will come when I allow it and not a moment before. And," he pressed his crotch against her center and rocked the firm ridge straining against his jeans, "I will fuck you when I'm good and ready. Right now, I'm mesmerized by these beauties."

"But—"

He cocked a dark eyebrow, seeming unmoved. "But nothing. You wanted to tangle with me. I'm a Dom, princess. You professed that you would do it my way. Was that a lie? Are you reneging?"

"Bloody hell. No, I'm not. Just... god... please hurry." She whimpered and bit her bottom lip as he wedged his big body more firmly between her spread thighs. The hard length of his desire dug into her pussy. Her panties were drenched. Her sex pulsed with lust.

And now he made more sense to her. He was a Dominant. She knew what BDSM was because some of the friends in her circle leaned in that direction. While she had never given any thought to whether it was something she would like, his commanding presence and the power he asserted were blinding.

The incendiary heat left her gobsmacked.

Flicking his tongue over the stiff peak of her nipple, squeezing the mounds in his hands, he murmured darkly, "I promise I will make you scream with pleasure; all you need to do is surrender your need to control. Trust that I will get you where you need to go."

She tugged at his plaid shirt. "I want this bloody thing off."

"Demanding little thing," he scolded with a lopsided grin, but he obliged her and rose up slightly to undo the buttons on his shirt. "And you broke the rule about touching me. I will give you a pass this time. Next time, I will spank that ass of yours for disobeying."

She helped him undress, greedy for skin-to-skin contact, tugging at the soft material. "Screw the blasted rules."

He chuckled softly, his eyes promising retribution for breaking his rule, and finished removing his shirt.

Fucking hell!

Her gaze soaked him up. Bianca had thought Mav was sexy with a shirt on. Without one? He was the hottest fucking bloke she had ever seen. She curled her fingers into her palms to keep herself from reaching out and caressing his defined pecs and abdominals. They were dusted with dark hair that narrowed into a single trail down his midsection and disappeared beneath his low-slung jeans.

He was rangy, with ropes of muscle piled on top of more muscle. He had wide shoulders, and defined arms, and his muscles rippled as he shifted. These muscles weren't made in a gym pumping iron, but from hard physical labor.

Her eyes dipped to the bulge straining against denim.

Oh good Christ, please let his cock be that big!

Maverick caught her lustful staring. The corners of his mouth curled up, his eyes chock-full of lascivious intent. He stepped back, relieving the erotic pressure at her core, and removed his boots one at a time. He kept his gaze on her while he unbuckled his belt, and undid the clasp on his jeans. The sound of his zipper lowering made goosebumps erupt over her skin. He shucked his jeans and stood before her in nothing but black boxer briefs.

Holy shit!

The thick bulge beneath those briefs had her biting her bottom lip. He wasn't just big, he was massive. She prayed he would fit. It had been ages since she had had sex with something that wasn't battery powered.

He fished a condom from his wallet before joining her back at the bed.

"Let's move you into the middle, princess," he murmured, lifting her up before she knew what he was about and depositing her in the dead center of the bed, with her head on the pillows.

He even took the time to move her hair out of the way. His gentleness was unexpected. And her stupid heart sighed at the act.

Maverick joined her in bed once he had her settled the way he wanted her, and placed the foil packet nearby for easy reach. Spreading her thighs wide, he situated his large form between them. Kneeling, he studied her, like he was contemplating the best method of torment to draw the naughty lovemaking out and make her squirm from erotic torture. Leaning forward, he propped his hands on the bed beside her shoulders and lowered his mouth. His chest hair teased her nipples.

Bianca was past the point of caring when she pleaded, "Maverick."

He swooped down and claimed her lips in a scintillating kiss, a hot tangle of tongues and teeth that left her shaky and needy. Good lord but the man had a talented mouth.

Bianca reached for him, needing to touch him, to feel those firm muscles under her fingertips. But he caught her hands before she could reach him and lifted them above her head to near the headboard. She strained against his hold. Potent desire slammed into her at being restrained, and she moaned into his mouth.

Maverick ended the kiss, his face stern, and said, "Keep your hands up where they are at. If you bring them down for any reason without my permission, I will spank that sweet ass of yours."

"What?" she sputtered, not mad really. Except... the thought of those big hands connecting with her butt, slapping it for being bad, had tendrils of liquid fire pulsing into her core. Did she want him to spank her?

He nipped her chin. "You heard me, princess. I told you I like it rough."

Oh god! She did want him to punish her and do all sorts of naughty, forbidden acts with her.

Maverick kissed his way down the slope of her chest to her boobs, and feasted. She didn't think she had ever had a man pay this much attention to them before. He suckled at the nipples, drawing them deep in the hot cavern of his mouth. He bit down on the buds again and again, until they were so stiff, they jutted and ached.

"Christ, I wish I had some nipple clamps on me. I would love to see how they look on you." He flicked his tongue over the abraded flesh, and slipped down her body.

Maverick hooked his thumbs under the waistband of her panties and drew them off. Tossing the slip of lace behind them, he parted her thighs even wider and stared at her pussy. His nostrils flared and he licked his lips, like he was anticipating the flavor of her cream.

He lowered his face, which was filled with carnal intent, pushing her thighs wider to accommodate the breadth of his shoulders. Using his thumbs, her parted her labia, and groaned.

"So wet for me already," he mumbled.

Before she could retort, he licked her crease from her clit all the way down to her forbidden channel and back up again. Gasping, she clutched at the headboard for something to hold onto. Maverick applied tongue and teeth to her sensitive flesh. Curling and flicking his tongue against the nub, he lapped at her sex until she writhed against his imprisoning hold.

She arched her back as pleasure swept her up. When she'd suggested they should have sex, she'd assumed it would be a quick tumble and then they would be done with it. She hadn't expected this drawn out, delicious agony, that would incinerate her from the inside out and obliterate the memory of all who came before him.

"Oh," she cried, undulating her hips.

He plunged his tongue deep inside her sheath, thrusting in and out. The first waves of her orgasm approached, coiling deep in her core. She wanted it. Needed the blissful oblivion.

Before she could climax, the dratted man backed off his relentless pace.

She whimpered. "Please."

His gaze lifted and connected with hers. "I told you, princess, you'll come when I'm ready for you to, and not a moment before."

Then he slipped a thick finger inside her pussy, leisurely thrusting it in and out. Her sex clenched around the digit. She rocked her hips, begging for more friction, but he held her steady as he plundered her depths, rubbing the sensitive pack of nerves inside her. He latched his mouth to her clit, sucking and nibbling on the bud, making it swell to painful proportions while he thrust his finger in long strokes.

He was going to drive her mad. And she was loving every dirty minute of it.

Moans spilled from her mouth.

Maverick added a second digit, stretching her sheath and pumping his fingers while he added a new element to his erotic torture—every time he thrust those fingers deep, once buried to the hilt inside her, he would spread them, stretching her channel, and would then retreat.

He increased the intensity of his thrusts until she was mindless with need. He bit down on her nub. A tidal wave of ecstasy slammed into her. Her back arched, her hips jerked as she climaxed, her cries echoing in the room.

"Oh god," she yelled at the tremors wracking her frame.

Before she had a chance to adjust, Maverick lifted her limp form. He shifted her body until she was on her hands and knees with her back to him. He positioned her hands on the headboard and said by her ear, "Keep your hands on the headboard."

The sound of the foil packet ripping made her pussy flutter. He crowded against her back. Spread her legs wide to accommodate him. The firm, broad crest of his cock pressed at her entrance until an inch of him was inside. She whimpered, needing more, needing everything.

Gripping her hips, he thrust and seated himself balls deep. He was huge, stretching her near the point of discomfort. Sparks showered through her. Clutching her hips tight, he shuttled his cock at a fast clip. Moans tumbled from her lips as she rocked back and met his powerful, earth-shattering thrusts with her own. She was awash in a sea of mindless pleasure. She adored the feel of his thick shaft stretching her to near the point of pain.

His large palm connected with her butt as he plunged deep. Her pussy fluttered and clenched at the hard whack. The pain slid deep inside her being and combined with the pleasure. She wanted more. She gasped at the heated flames that engulfed her.

A smack fell on the other butt cheek and she howled, slamming her hips back.

He grunted as he fucked her. His palm smacked her ass again and again as he hammered her channel. Then he leaned forward, his hands slid up her ribcage, and he cupped her tits. He pummeled her sheath in hard brutal strokes that walked the line of violence. He pinched and kneaded her breasts. His harsh breaths and grunts filled her ears.

She was loving every wicked second of it.

Her sex fluttered—she was nearing the point of no return and the ecstasy her body craved.

Maverick pulled out.

"No! Are you bloody trying to make me hurt you?" She wailed at the emptiness.

His dark laugh made her blood boil. Then he was turning her around. He knelt on the bed and positioned her facing him so that she was straddling his thighs. "I want you to pretend you're riding Sunshine, princess. I've had fantasies all week watching you ride her, now I want you to ride me."

"You're being a dick," she said, and internally cursed that she sounded pouty.

"No, you want my dick in that pretty little cunt of yours, and you want all the control too. That's not going to happen. Surrender, princess."

"Never."

A sexy smirk spread over his lips. "You will."

Then, without warning, he furrowed inside her, and left her gasping at the waves of pleasure. Maverick held her close, and wrapped her legs around his waist. In this position, their torsos were aligned. The whorls of his chest hair abraded her sensitive nipples. Those big, firm hands gripped her bottom and moved her with his thrusts.

She mewled unintelligible sounds.

Circling her arms around his neck, she locked her gaze with his and began to undulate, thrusting down as he thrust up. This new angle of penetration hit all her nerve endings as he slid deeper with each thrust. In no time she was writhing and quaking at her impending release.

But then he shifted her onto her back, never once breaking the connection or withdrawing from her sheath, until he was propped on his elbows and plowing her pussy with such force, every plunge left her moaning uncontrollably.

She had asked him to fuck her brains out. Whelp, the cowboy was delivering in spades.

Pressing her into the mattress, his face hovered above hers, and he jackhammered inside her. Her fingers clung to his back; dug into the hard muscles. The pleasure built in such a way that she knew she could no longer hold onto any control. If he wanted it all, he could have it. She was done with it all, and so she simply let go.

It was the most freeing moment of her existence.

And it was in that moment, their lovemaking turned downright feral—like he sensed her willing surrender. Maverick buried his face against her neck and pistoned his hips. They clung together as they raced toward bliss.

He slammed home, and she broke apart.

"Maverick," she sobbed as she came. Shockwaves crashed over her in rapid succession. She quaked in his arms as her pussy spasmed around his plunging cock. Distantly, she felt him strain and his hips jerk. His cock jolted within the clutching walls of her channel.

"Ah, fuck," he groaned, and pummeled inside her as he came. He thrust through the climax, drawing the pleasure out for them until they were left with only aftershocks and bliss.

They stayed that way, wrapped in one another, the rapid-fire beat of their hearts pounding against their chests. Out of everything that had happened tonight, Bianca had never expected a slice of intimacy with him. And truthfully, she liked the way he felt, snug between her thighs, covering her body. It made her feel warm and protected—and in some way, cherished—that he didn't roll off her the second he'd climaxed like so many guys did.

It could have been ten seconds or ten minutes before he shifted his big body and lifted his head.

She opened her eyes and found him contemplating her, with concern dotting his brow.

"No regrets?" he asked.

"None. That was the best bad decision I've ever made. I..." She nibbled on her bottom lip and stopped herself from asking outright.

"What? Spit it out, princess."

"Well, I was just wondering how many more bad decisions I could make tonight—depending on your recovery skills, that is."

His stare turned downright carnal.

"Oh, I think you're about to find out. From here on out tonight, you will address me as Sir, and your safeword is *red*. Got it, princess?" He took her mouth in a heated exchange that left her gasping and unable to reply.

As it happened, Maverick helped her make three more bad decisions that night. All told, Bianca thought she should have started making bad decisions years ago.

11

*H*e stayed the night.

Maverick never spent the night with a woman after sex. It was far too intimate. He liked his space and his freedom. And he preferred keeping a safe emotional distance.

He hadn't planned on sleeping here, nor had his surprise bed partner asked him to. Sometime after their fourth go around, they had crashed beside each other from sheer exhausted bliss. He glanced at the smooth lines of her slim back, which was facing his way. The golden waves of her silken hair were spread out behind her on the pale blue pillow.

When he had come upon her last night, sitting barefoot on the steps, looking defeated, there had been a shift inside him. Instead of wanting to rile her up, watch her cheeks flush with anger and annoyance as she primly looked down her nose at him, he had wanted to offer comfort. And then she had raised her face, a desolate expression filling her goddess eyes, and all he'd wanted to do was gather her close to chase away the darkness eating at her.

It was that urge that had him agreeing to a drink.

He understood that expression. It was one he had seen in the mirror all too often growing up.

When she'd suggested they should have sex, he'd been rock hard in an instant. To say that she had shocked him was the understatement of the century.

He'd refused... at first.

He really wasn't sure he liked her. Just because he had imagined what she looked like naked, that didn't mean a thing. He was a guy, and one who adored the female form.

But then she'd removed her blouse and revealed those pillowy breasts. He'd been struck dumb. The plump mounds looked like a gift in the white lace bra. In an instant, all his meticulous control had dissolved as desire overrode his system.

And when he had gotten her back into the bedroom and removed the bra, he'd nearly creamed in his pants like an unschooled teen getting to second base for the first time. Maverick had seen, fondled, and sucked on his fair share of tits: small, large, pointed, and rounded, those with small blush nipples, and those with big, dusky, round areolas.

But without a doubt, Bianca had the most gorgeous set of breasts ever. Full, round, with rose-tipped nipples that beseeched his hungry mouth. He could spend hours worshiping them—and had, for the better part of the night.

He would love to take her to Cabin X; see how they looked bound, with clamps squeezing the nipples.

His dick stirred at the erotic imagery.

Whoa! Down, boy.

Last night was a once and done deal. He didn't do repeats. Ever. That way lay attachment city and eventual heartbreak. He had experienced enough of that for multiple lifetimes.

Noting the time on the bedside clock, he rose. If he was going to make it home, shower, and arrive at the stables on time for another full day, he didn't have much of a choice.

He slid out of bed. His unexpected bed partner rolled over. With her eyes cracked open a slit, she scowled and said, "There'd better be a good reason that you're getting up this bloody early."

Pulling his boxers and jeans on, he shrugged as he zipped his jeans. "Need to get ready for work."

"Ah, well then. Thanks for everything. If you could lock the front door on your way out, I would appreciate it ever so much, because some of us are going back to bed," she said, and stretched so that those breasts of hers looked like they were about to break free of their covering beneath the sheet. The same breasts he had the urge to mark—well, more than he already had. By the third or fourth go around, it all grew rather hazy—they had been all hot hands and mouths, and he might have left behind a mark or two.

But he wanted to cover those plump mounds with his brand.

Bianca snuggled underneath the covers and rolled away from him. Her response made it sound as if last night had been a transaction between them, instead of the carnal indulgences tour they had made of each other's bodies.

Picking his plaid up off the floor, he donned the wrinkled shirt, confused by her actions.

Except... this was how he wanted it with his bed partners, whether unexpected or not, right? He shoved his boots on. It was what he always wanted where women were concerned, so why in holy hell was he... hurt that he wasn't garnering more of a reaction? Most women would at least make playful attempts to tug him back into bed on his way out the door, for an erotic sendoff. But not this one, nope, she was too cool for anything like that. And if he hadn't tasted her intoxicating fire last night, he'd believe she was a block of ice. But he knew better.

Still, her response—or lack of one—knocked him off his center of gravity. "Whatever you say, princess. See you at your last riding lesson."

He picked his hat up off the floor in the kitchen on his way and flipped the lock on the door as he headed out. Unsettled, he climbed into his truck and drove to his place.

One of the nice things about working for the ranch was they had cabins and living spaces for each employee, away from the main hotel and cabin hub, as part of their salary. The seasonal people garnered spots in the bunkhouse. But as head wrangler, Mav had been given one of the available cabins, and it had been home for almost a decade. Living on ranch property made the commute much easier, especially during winter when the area was battered with snow and winter weather.

His two-bedroom cabin was located in a secluded grove of pine trees. The walnut wood blended in with the scenery. While there was a small, two-stall barn attached where he could house Black Jack, it was easier to board him at the ranch stables.

This place was home—for now.

Until he had saved enough to build his place on the land he had purchased from the ranch. The cost of buying it had removed a good chunk of his savings. But it was worth it, to own land that belonged to him and couldn't be taken away.

He stomped into his cabin, which was similar in design to the guest cabins, only larger. There was much more space in the living room, a larger dining area, and a much bigger kitchen, which was helpful in the winter months. Sighing, he stripped off his boots by the front door to keep from tracking dirt all over the place, wishing he had a mudroom. That was one addition to the house he would build he planned to include. He dropped his hat, keys, and wallet on the oak kitchen table, noting the dishes in the rack by the sink that needed to be stowed away. It was a chore he'd have to do later. He started the coffee pot. While that was brewing, he trod into the bathroom, stripped out of his used clothes, tossing them in the overly full hamper, and stepped into the shower.

Under the warm spray, he struggled to get his head back on straight. Bianca's indifferent response this morning bothered him. Like he sought validation of his usefulness in the only way he had ever allowed it to matter—in the bedroom.

And when she'd dismissed him... he rubbed at the ache in his chest. He didn't understand why her lack of enthusiasm rattled him this much. Likely because it *never* happened. Not once since he had entered the lifestyle and applied himself in the art of making a woman scream with untold pleasure had there been a woman to so easily dismiss him from her bed.

Granted, it was possible that she was exhausted, given the number of rounds they had gone. If he had a choice between staying in bed or heading into work, he would still be in bed, with Bianca.

That thought made him feel somewhat more at ease.

It didn't eliminate the negative doubt, the one that told him he was worthless and would never amount to a thing. That he was only good for causing other people hardship.

He slammed the door on thoughts of his past. When he'd kicked off the dust of his hometown at eighteen and began eking out a life he could take pride in, Maverick had promised himself that his past was done. It was useless dragging out the torrid, unhappy business. He had moved around a bit, worked at various ranches over multiple States, learning everything he could, until he landed at Silver Springs ten years ago. Colt had taken a chance on him, hiring him as head wrangler.

Through tenacity and grit, he had carved a life for himself here.

He considered Colt, Emmett, Tanner, Lincoln, Noah, and Duncan his brothers. The brothers he had always wished for growing up. They were the ones who introduced him to the lifestyle.

And he had applied himself to learning the ropes of being a Dominant much like he had with studying to become the best damn wrangler west of the Mississippi. The women in town knew that he was the guy to call when they wanted a good time between the sheets.

He shut the water off and stepped out.

Mav wasn't certain when the idea of that, carrying that label, had begun to change for him. But it was part of the reason behind his dry spell when it came to bed partners.

Until last night.

Mav dressed for the day, poured coffee into a travel mug, and swore when he noticed the time. He'd call the restaurant and beg them to deliver a breakfast burrito to the stables for him. Shoving his phone and wallet in his pocket, he grabbed his keys and headed out.

He arrived at the stables, and stopped in his office first to go over the employee schedule today. Noah was going to be arriving with stock to switch out. Mav would have Billy and David work on readying the twenty horses that would be heading for their three-week vacation at stable number two, which was located away from the main hub. They were pretty original around here with naming things. The main stable was designated stable one. They tended to shorten it down to *one* or *two* when talking about the different stables.

With the number of horses in their herd, rotating them in and out ensured that the horses weren't overtaxed and hopefully did not fall to injury. While they were at stable two, they grazed and grew fat as they relaxed after taking riders on trail rides.

Each horse was on a six weeks on the job and three weeks off rotation. Each week, another bit of stock was swapped out. It worked for them, and kept the horses healthy and happy, although it was a ton of paperwork. They had to make sure fresh stalls were prepped for the new stock arriving, ready the stock heading to the back stables, clean the stalls they left behind. Make sure the vitals, diet restrictions, vitamin supplements and the like for each horse were brought up to date if there were any changes since they were on duty last. Send any concerns along about the stock heading out of rotation.

As workers poked their heads into his office, Mav gave them their assignments for the day. He managed a few bites of his burrito before it was time to begin feeding the horses. Then they all had to be groomed and checked over for any ailments before being added to the schedule as a rider for the day.

Before he realized it, the morning had gotten away from him, like it did most days.

In the middle of saddling Titus, for Jamie's trail ride group, it struck him. Bianca hadn't come down for their final riding lesson. Between the trade off on the stock, and number of balls he'd ended up juggling, Mav had subsequently forgotten.

Once Titus was saddled and Jamie had his group in hand, Maverick headed toward the front desk.

"Marlie, did Miss Peabody come in for her riding lesson?" he asked.

Marlie was a mother of three teenagers, and liked to say her job here kept her sane enough to deal with the hooligans she had birthed. The ranch would be lost without her. She handled the bulk majority of bookings, took care of customer payments and complaints. She shook her head and looked up from her computer. "Nope. She never showed. Do you want me to call her cabin?"

"Not necessary. The day just got away from me and I wondered if she had ever made it. Thanks, though. If you need me, I will be in my office, trying to catch up on paperwork."

"No worries, boss. We're good here."

Maverick nodded and strode off, fishing his phone from his back pocket. Back in his office, he brought up Bianca's cabin information, which had her cell number listed. He called her, dialing the number. Her cultured voice with the British accent filtered through the receiver in a recording that told him to leave a message and she would return his call.

"Miss Peabody, you skipped your riding lesson. If you are not going to appear for a scheduled event, please contact the stables twenty-four hours in advance. As it is, ranch policy dictates that we will be forced to charge you for the lesson. Please call the stables if you have any questions."

He hung up, proud of himself that he had sounded level headed and professional in the message—when what he really wanted to ask her was: what the fuck? And discover why she had skipped out on the lesson.

Was she embarrassed they had spent the night together? Did she regret it even though she had said differently?

He didn't regret it. She had been a fucking sensual revelation. And there was a naughty submissive lurking beneath the posh layers.

As he attacked the paperwork piling up on his desk, he told himself it didn't matter. She could be avoiding him, and have decided she didn't want to ride anymore except for trail rides. But that line of thought brought back the memory of last night, when she had ridden him like a cowgirl, those big, beautiful globes jiggling enticingly.

He shifted in his chair and swore at the firm press of his erection. Damn greedy bastard had seen more action last night than he had all last month.

It didn't matter why she'd skipped the lesson. Just because his conquests normally returned the next day, seeking to cast their net and catch him a second time, only for him to smile and send them on their way, pining for more... In a sick, twisted sense, those responses had made him feel valued.

Bianca's avoidance, combined with her reaction—or lack of one—this morning reopened the desolate void inside him. The one that reminded him he had never been worth a damn thing. So much so, he could hear the deep timbre of his father's voice as he told Maverick that, just like him, he was fated to have his life amount to a pile of horse manure, trapped in a marriage neither party wanted but couldn't escape, and the sooner he reconciled himself to that reality, the better off he would be.

But it still didn't answer his question. Why had she treated last night as if it hadn't meant a thing to her?

The riddle eluded him, but he intended to find out.

---

12

*B*right sunlight streaming across her pillow pulled Bianca from the deepest, most restful night of sleep she had experienced in years.

Stretching, she glanced beside her at the empty space and couldn't help but bury her nose in the pillow he'd used. She could smell him, the lingering scents of leather and alpha man. Her stomach fluttered and her sex rippled at the memory of those hands roving over her body.

Without a doubt, sex with Maverick had led to the most erotic night of her life.

Her body felt bruised and sore, but the multiple climaxes had been worth it. And Maverick had the stamina of half a dozen men. He might have hesitated at first, but when he committed to a course of action, god, the results were bloody fantastic.

Bianca climbed out of bed and padded into the bathroom. In the mirror, she caught sight of her body. There were bruises on her hips from where he had held her tight and banged her senseless. Beneath each nipple was a sizeable hickey, not to mention her nipples were raw and abraded. The man had adored her breasts.

She laughed, clasping her hands over her mouth as she cut loose.

She couldn't remember the last time she had felt this deep in the bone good. In the shower, she sang off key, nigh to bursting with euphoria. After her shower, she slipped on jeans and a white tank top before heading into the kitchen.

She cooked. Well, to be fair, she boiled two eggs to go with her muffin and fruit. It really didn't constitute as cooking. The weather was pleasant, so she carried her breakfast and coffee out onto the front porch to sit in one of the Adirondack chairs. There was a slight chill in the breeze, but it was refreshing.

The morning was gloriously sun kissed. Inspired, Bianca retrieved one of her sketchpads and drew while she ate. Energized after last night, she illustrated sketch after sketch until the tide built inside her and the picture rose into a chokehold of what she needed to get on canvas.

Bianca carted everything back into the cabin, not even bothering to lock the front door because she was too intent on the creativity surging inside. She laid her dishes in the sink. They could be dealt with later.

The scene bubbled and brewed as it blotted out reality. In her studio, she placed a fresh canvas on the easel, and didn't even bother with the paint smock. Bianca crafted her palette of colors and set her brushes at the ready.

And then she was off to the races, immersed in the colors and form as the vision bloomed to life. Her brush strokes feathered here, glided there. She changed brushes and colors, mixing some together, furiously working to transfer what was in her mind and heart onto canvas. Her soul sang as she submerged herself in the deep end, all her focus trained on the artwork.

Her artwork.

She poured her being into the shape and design. Before she knew it, grass appeared, then trees, mountains, and clouds scuttling over the peaks. The drive pushed her to complete it before the image in her mind dissolved.

When she was finished, panting from the rush, she stepped back, pressing a hand to her chest. It was the view outside the cabin with the sun rising, turning the world golden.

But even then, she wasn't done. It was like last night, being here, being with him, the passion that had been unleashed inside her had tossed open the floodgates of her creativity.

Wave upon wave crashed into her. She picked another blank canvas, starting anew with the vision burning in her mind.

Bianca painted and sketched, then painted some more. At some point, she put the radio on with classical playing the background. Not everyone enjoyed classical music, but it was one of her favorite genres—Beethoven, Brahms, Chopin, Mozart, Bach, and more.

She stopped for a brief spot of dinner, mainly because she was starved and had not eaten since morning. She sketched while dinner heated up in the microwave. It was a picture of Maverick as he had stood over her, naked, erect, his gaze carnal and intent lewd.

She stuffed her face quickly as another image flashed into her brain. She didn't even finish her food and left it half eaten on the table, in too much of a hurry to return to her creations.

Bianca stood before a new canvas, music pumping out

of the radio as she glided her paint brush over the scene. In no time, she became lost in her creation. She felt more like herself than she had in years. The stables and paddock began to come into focus as she moved her brush. Short strokes, long glides as the white canvas disappeared beneath the profusion of color and Mozart blasted through the speakers.

A hand fell upon her shoulder. "Ah!"

What the fuck!

She jolted. The paintbrush flipped out of her hand and landed on the floor with a wet splat, making her infinitely thankful she'd had the foresight to lay down drop cloths over the hardwood.

With her heart in her chest pounding rapidly, she swiveled around just as Maverick shut off the radio. The sudden deafening silence competed with the racing beat of her heart. The man looked all big and badass in his jeans and red plaid. Did he own *anything* that wasn't denim and plaid? There was a deep scowl on his face, like he was miffed at her.

She asked, "What the bloody hell, Maverick? Are you trying to scare ten years off my life?"

"I was worried when you didn't show up at the stables today for your ride." His hands were planted on his lean hips while he glared, a muscle ticking in his strong jaw.

She was uncertain that was the real reason, given his stance, until she spotted desire and a flash of insecurity in those golden eyes. The rugged cowboy was utterly adorable. He had been worried about more than just her missing the ride. It made her wonder if his whole being a Dominant thing was a shield he used to keep women at bay. She didn't mind the kinkier aspects of what they'd done last night. In fact, she would like to do it again, and even try things she had always been too afraid to try.

"I've been busy." She jerked her chin toward the finished canvases and wiped her hands on a cloth to remove the paint splotches covering them, not worried at all that her manicure was chipped. It was the first time in forever that she wasn't concerned that gossip would abound if she wasn't fully decked out and impeccable in her appearance.

"I can see that." His gaze slid over each painting propped up and drying before slanting intensely back her way.

She bent, picked up the fallen paintbrush, and dipped it in her water bucket to clean it, eyeing the rangy man. An air of barely leashed danger surrounded him.

"You've got paint all over you, princess."

He was good at pretending he wasn't affected, she would give him that. But he couldn't conceal his lust for her any longer. Not any more than she could ignore the tugging curls of heat spiraling in her belly at his proximity. After their acrobatics last night, she'd figured he had slaked his thirst and would move on.

Bianca hadn't been lying when she'd told him she didn't want promises. Pledges of any kind tended to place shackles upon a person. She was enjoying her freedom far too much to consider anything resembling commitment.

Not that she could commit to him even if she wanted to, given the... ahem, engagement.

Although, she wouldn't say no to having him in her bed again. Because lord love a duck, she would enjoy another sensual bout with the marathon man.

Feeling a bit devilish, she dipped her fingertips into the blue and red paint on her color palette. When she'd determined there was a good enough amount coating the tips, she approached him, her bottom lip between her teeth and her intent clear as day on her face.

He cocked a brow, his gaze lasering in on her chest and hips as she put some extra sway into her progression. "What do you think you're doing?"

"Finger painting," she said, and traced a finger coated in sky blue paint down his stubble covered cheek.

His eyes darkened. "I'm warning you now, princess, you keep it up, I will punish you."

"Promise?" she asked. Because she wanted to push him over the edge and watch him snap. Then he'd take her, put his hands on her again. And as need gushed inside her, she knew she would expire if he didn't touch her. Bianca took her index finger coated in bright, fire engine red paint, and made a dot on the tip of his nose, giving a *boop* sound.

His gaze narrowed. "Don't say you didn't ask for it."

Before she could react, he caught her hand in his, lifted it, and smeared the remaining paint on her fingers down her cheek. She squealed, trying to fight his hold as he laughed, the rich, deep sound of his chuckles filled her chest.

The action ignited a frenzy. They went a little wild after that. Each grabbed paint from her palette and smeared it over the other. And then his mouth latched onto hers. She gripped his shirt as he ate at her mouth. Her mewls of desire were silenced by his lips.

God, the man could kiss.

Desire battered them. Hands tugged and yanked at clothing until they were both gloriously nude. They fought for purchase on the hardwood floor covered by the drop cloth and spattered with drops of paint. His mouth surrounded a distended nipple and sucked hard on the bud. Her back arched at the ecstasy. She threaded her hands into his hair, unmindful of the fact that she still had paint on them.

They were greedy and desperate as heat rose in seismic waves, obliterating all else.

And then he was pushing inside her, all nine solid inches. She had been empty, and now she was full. It was everything—*he* was everything—she needed. She clawed at his back as he thrust deep inside—so deep, it was as if he became an indelible part of her. It was more than she had ever believed she might feel. She didn't understand why he had the ability to electrify her and blot out the rest of the world until she was consumed by him, until nothing but him moving, thrusting, pumping deep as she writhed and met him, became the focal point of her world.

Last night had been an acrobatic dance. Tonight, it was pedal to the metal, no holds barred fucking. It was gritty, dirty need. Their bodies fused together, crashing together like a storm. Pleasure spiraled with each hurried thrust, every stroke and plunge.

"Come for me, princess," Maverick groaned. "I want to hear you scream."

He pistoned inside her. Bianca clung, undulating as his cock thrust and sent her hurtling over the ledge. She detonated.

"Fuck!" she keened, and quaked within his firm grasp. Her pussy fluttered and clutched at his plunging staff.

"Oh, fuck." He rammed his dick in her cunt and strained. His cock jerked as he roared his completion, fucking her furiously, ensuring they imbibed every drop of ecstasy from their climaxes.

While she was still rippling around his shaft with aftershocks, he lifted his head and started laughing. Lifting her gaze, she realized he wasn't laughing at her but at them. They had got paint everywhere. Absolutely *everywhere*.

She laughed until tears streamed down her face. "Perhaps we should go get in the shower."

"Is that an invitation?"

"Actually, it's a demand. You have paint marks shaped like my boobs on your chest."

"And whose fault is that?"

"I didn't think you would make it an all-out war. Although, I can't say I mind the outcome at all." She wriggled her hips.

With a devilish grin on his lips, he murmured, "You started it. I was just obliging you. And I still haven't punished you for it either."

"And how do you plan on doing that?"

Maverick shifted, withdrawing from her body. "I'll show you, I... oh shit, please tell me you're on the pill." Remorse filling his gaze, he said, "I'm sorry, I've never forgotten a condom before."

It was the first time for her as well, and she hadn't even noticed the lack. Proof that the moment he touched her, she lost all ability to think.

"Relax cowboy, I'm on the pill and clean, so no worries on this end," she said, trying to alleviate his obvious guilt.

"Still, it wasn't right of me to forget that way."

She shrugged. "We both got carried away. I honestly didn't notice you hadn't put one on."

"Why? Are you used to having men not wear them? Is that a British thing?" he asked as he sat up.

"I didn't say that. That was the first time I've ever had sex without protection."

"Is it really?" Pleasure filled his eyes as he pulled her up into a sitting position beside him.

"Yes. Now, we should head into the shower and wash the paint off before it dries completely."

"It's a first for me as well, and was unintentional on my part," he said, rather seriously.

Laying her palm against his cheek, his short stubble scraping her hand, she brushed her lips over his and said, "Well, perhaps next time, you can purposely not wear one so we can both feel the full effect, since we sort of lost our heads back there."

His gaze turned downright primal. "We can do that. But first, I will show you just how thorough we are out here in the Rockies, at washing every nook and cranny."

He rose, hoisted her into his arms in a way that had her laughing, and carried her into the bathroom.

13

*H*e had taken her without a condom.

What the fuck had he been thinking?

That thought blared through his brain as he walked them into her bathroom. He didn't stop until they stood in the shower stall, where he gently lowered her onto her feet and switched the water on. He had come inside her without any barrier. Christ, it was like he had branded her on the inside.

A part of him was panicking, worried that he might have gotten her pregnant, and was following in the same footsteps of his old man. However, on the flip side, the Dom part of him loved that he'd spilled inside her, and craved the chance to do it again.

Maverick was fucking careful—as in, he didn't dip his dick until he was wearing a slicker. But Bianca did something to him. Maybe it was finding her with paint smeared along one cheek and blotches of it on her tank. Perhaps it had been the naughty joy in her eyes as she'd approached him with her fingers covered in paint.

Because in that moment, the prim and proper miss had

been replaced by a siren, drawing him in, until his heartbeat thundered, and his dick ached for the hot clasp of her cunt. From the moment he spied her there, he'd been entranced, and rock hard, waiting on a sign from her that an advance would be welcomed. And when she drew her paint-coated finger down his cheek, he'd gone berserk, desperate to be inside her.

In the shower, they helped each other scrub paint from their bodies.

Her lush form beckoned him. When they were reasonably paint free, he stepped into her, backing her up against the tile wall.

"What are you doing?" she asked nervously, her blue eyes dilated with desire.

He was a sick, sick man for enjoying the sadistic thrill of making her nervous and wonder what he would do with her next. He planned to take her again. This time, he would pay attention to the feel of her cunt squeezing him bareback. His cock jolted at the thought. Earlier, they had been too wrapped up in each other, too deeply enmeshed, so the lack of one hadn't even registered.

It should worry him, the seductive hold she had on him.

But any concern he felt flittered away as he watched the unsteady rise and fall of her fucking knockout tits. He cupped them in his hands, his thumbs circling and rubbing over the taut peaks.

"What does it look like I'm doing?"

Her breath hitched when he squeezed the nipples and rolled them; her eyes went blurry with pleasure.

He lowered himself to his knees and parted her thighs, lifting one slim leg up over his shoulder. The move gave him direct access to her puffy pink sex, the labia swollen from their last entanglement. But he needed to taste her, see if her flavor was different with his spunk inside her.

"Maverick," she gasped when he swiped his tongue along her crease.

"I thought I told you last night to call me Sir when we were like this, or did you forget?"

"No, Sir."

His fingers toyed with her slit, circling her clit. "Good. You're not allowed to come until I say you can."

"What? That's insane. I don't know that I can," she whimpered, and shook her head.

"You'll do it because it pleases me," he demanded, not giving her any quarter to refuse his request. Because he had spied a submissive buried within her. And the thought of bringing her out, letting the submissive surface, and hand her power over—fuck. He needed it.

At his command, her demeanor visibly shifted. She softened both face and form in her need to satisfy him. It was fucking intoxicating. She was submitting and didn't even realize it.

Bianca nodded. "Yes, Sir."

At her compliance, he lapped at her cunt. He took his time, studying her every response to each flick of his tongue. Her hands gripped his hair and her body trembled. And she tasted like honey. When he slipped his tongue in her sheath, thrusting in and out, he growled at tasting himself there, mixed with her cream. His cock jerked and lengthened.

She whimpered, her mouth hung open, and she rocked against his thrusting tongue.

He drove her body up toward the first shuddering peak of climax before he backed off.

Since he had slaked the most urgent parts of his lust, this time wasn't going to be fast or over until he was ready.

He licked at her until her leg could no longer hold her. Then he rose, shut the water off, and carried her out of the shower. Taking a towel from the rack, he dried them both off, unmindful of his erection. He was more intent on the woman he planned to make come, screaming his name.

But she surprised him. She always seemed to be doing that. Perhaps that was where some of his fascination originated from.

Bianca slipped to her knees on the bathroom rug and gripped his dick in her delicate hands. The woman didn't even ask for his permission, just enveloped his shaft in her hot little mouth. She took him deep, her gaze on his face as she bobbed up and down. He hissed at the pleasure building. He cupped her head in his hands, canting his hips as he fucked her mouth.

He watched his shaft disappear as she cupped his balls, rolling them in her hand.

The hedonism grew to be too much, his need for gratification shook the lock on his control. He didn't want to ejaculate in her mouth. Not this time. Next time. He wanted to empty his payload inside her hot cunt.

Why did he think there would be a next time?

Shoving the weird thought aside, he pulled out of her mouth. She peered up at him, her gaze full of lust. Mav lifted her onto her feet and claimed her lips in a heady tangle. But the desire to feel her pussy clench around his shaft became overwhelming. Tearing his mouth off hers, he moved her over to the vanity with the long mirror attached to it. He bent her over at the waist and placed her hands on the counter.

"Keep your eyes open and focused on me. I want you to watch me fuck you."

She moaned and nodded her compliance.

Spreading her thighs, he bent his knees slightly to achieve the perfect angle since she was half a foot shorter, then lined his cock up with her pussy entrance. Pressing the tip inside, unencumbered by latex, he gripped her hips in his hands.

"Eyes on me," he ground out through clenched teeth at the feel of her slick heat.

Then he thrust, plunging deep in a single stroke, until he was buried inside her. Her gasp of pleasure fueled him.

Bareback, good Christ!

He fought against the waves of pleasure, his need to control their mating just as powerful as his need for release. It took him a moment to lasso himself under control. Her cunt was hotter than any he had been inside. And without the latex barrier, he felt every distinct flutter as she clenched around him as if greedy to keep him there.

With his gaze locked on hers, he withdrew until only the tip remained, and slammed back inside with a grunt. He established a brutal pace. Her tits swayed and jiggled as he pounded her. She gritted her teeth, and thrust back against him.

It was fucking hot as hell—better than any other woman he had slept with, and that was saying something. Over the years, he had played the field with relish. And he wasn't going to last, not with the way she squeezed him tight.

"Let go and surrender. Come for me, princess." He snaked his arm around her hip and found her swollen clit, giving it a few good fast rubs.

Her moans echoed in the space. He shuttled his shaft, pounding deep, and was rewarded with the violent, squeezing spasms of her cunt as she came. Her mouth dropped open as a long, low moan came out.

He unleashed his control. Holding her hips steady, he fucked her, until his climax neared and hit like a sonic boom. One minute, he was on the precipice. The next, he shot his load, coming long and hard, his knees shaking at the force.

When she sagged and began to sink down against the vanity, he scooped her into his arms and carried her to bed where, for the second night in a row, he did something completely out of character. He stayed, and he held her. Wrapped up in her form, he slept the sleep of the dead.

14

*T*wo days later, Mav was assessing the tack room supplies, determining what could be repaired and what needed to be replaced, when he heard the cultured accent.

Maverick hadn't seen Bianca since he left her place two days prior in clothing stained with paint. The woman had spun his world. It was a bit like riding a bucking bronco and he had just lost his grip, falling through the air, worried those hooves might kick him on the way down, but he still hadn't landed in the dirt yet.

And the wildness of it had made him lose his head a bit —enough so that when he had woken with her body plastered around him, he hadn't found the strength to walk away. His dick lengthened at the soft press of her breasts. Maverick woke her up with his mouth latched around a pert, rosy nipple, and his fingers stroking through her cleft. Then she had clutched at him as he'd driven inside, and their lovemaking had been over far too quickly.

But when he left her cabin that morning, he'd felt like he had been punched in the stomach at the softer emotions she drew out of him. Maverick couldn't develop a case on her. It wasn't even remotely practical, let alone smart. She was a visitor—not just to the state, but the whole dang country.

Drawn to her like there was an invisible cord connecting them, he left the tack room, his task forgotten, and headed toward the front.

"Yes, if Sunshine is available, I would love to take her out on a trail ride for an hour or two."

"I'm not sure we have the staff available, Miss Peabody. Let me check and see if any of the wranglers are available," Marlie commented.

Mav rounded the corner, assessing Bianca in those skin-tight jeans and the ivory riding top with a protective vest. She had added the soft blue bucket hat to her head, with—Jesus Christ, he was doomed—her hair in pigtails, the glossy waves of golden hair falling over her chest. "I'm available to take Miss Peabody for a ride, Marlie. It's nearing my lunch break anyway," he said.

Bianca's face swiveled in his direction. A rosy flush crept up her neck and into her cheeks as she stared at him. The memory of the two of them filled her eyes. And there was a distinct flicker of carnal longing. She wanted him.

"Oh, but you don't have to miss your lunch." Her breathy reply blasted desire through his body.

He would fucking starve if it meant he got to feel the hot vise grip of her cunt around his cock again. "It's just a sandwich, princess, and not the first time I will eat my lunch on the trail. Do you want to ride, or not?"

He let the dark insinuation linger in the air. As much as he had told himself to stay away from her, it would take putting him six feet under to steer him off his course. And even then, he might just rise from the dead for a chance to have her again.

Her pupils dilated and her breath hitched. "No. I want to ride."

Victory and pleasure rushed through him. He nodded. "Good. Mark me out in the book for the next two hours," he said to Marlie. Then, to Bianca, "Come with me, princess."

He jerked his head. With her lush bottom lip caught between her teeth, she walked beside him back to Sunshine's stall.

"Really Maverick, I don't want you to have to miss your break," she said as Sunshine stuck her head over the stall and nudged her chest playfully. Those two had really bonded.

He tilted his head. "Are you ashamed to be seen with me, princess?"

"What? No, of course not." She seemed like she was going to say more but stopped herself.

He stepped into her space until she had to tilt her face up to look him in the eyes.

"It's something. Tell me," he murmured with an edge of steel behind his words.

"I just figured you had other things to do and didn't want to be bothered." She glanced away, but not before he spied hurt in her eyes.

A slow, seductive grin split his face. "You missed me, princess."

"I don't know what you're talking about."

He chuckled as a weight seemed to lift from his shoulders. "Keep on telling yourself that. I apologize for not stopping by the last two nights. We had a sick mare that needed round the clock care. Otherwise..." He drifted off, letting the innuendo linger that he would have appeared on her doorstep for another repeat performance.

And surprisingly, if Glory hadn't been ill, he *would* have stopped at Bianca's cabin.

It wasn't like him at all. But he couldn't deny that she entranced him. This need he had for her was a force of nature that he figured he needed to play out until it sputtered and died. It captivated him how she could appear cold and distant—until he got his hands on her. And then she transformed into a blazing inferno that flayed him open and left him awash in ecstasy.

"Is the mare all right?"

Her concern for the horse warmed him. "She is, thankfully. If you need a restroom, now's the time, while I get Sunshine and Black Jack saddled."

She retreated. "I'll be right back."

He watched her head to the restroom before he strode over to the tack room, and got a saddle and supplies for Sunshine. He had just finished buckling the saddle when Bianca returned to the stall.

He handed her the reins and said, "Wait here while I get Black Jack saddled."

"Sure," she said, and turned her attention to Sunshine. Her low murmurs and endearments toward the mare stirred him something fierce.

Hell, *she* stirred him.

And he couldn't seem to find his balance. Normally, once he had tumbled with a woman, the allure that attracted him vanished. But with Bianca, it continued to increase at exponential rates, and if he wasn't careful, he would grow attached. In short order, she had become an addiction, she was in his blood. And he feared his feelings went deeper, but wasn't ready or willing to examine that further.

Once Mav had Black Jack saddled, he tossed his sandwich in his saddle bag, along with some water, and led him from the stall. The stallion pranced out into the open space.

"It has been a while since we went on a nice ride, hasn't it, bud?" Mav patted his neck as they joined Bianca and Sunshine.

Bianca glanced at Jack. "Who is this handsome devil?"

She held out a hand to Jack, who was always one to impress the ladies. He nudged her hand and let her pet him.

"This is Black Jack. Say hello to Bianca, Jack," he commanded.

Jack executed a gentlemanly bow that had her laughing. "Such a gentleman."

"Oh, he's like any other guy; likes to show off for the ladies. Stay, Jack," Mav ordered the stallion. "Let's get you mounted up."

Maverick cupped his hands and lifted Bianca onto the saddle. His hands lingered longer than necessary. Christ, she made him yearn and hunger for more than he ever had with another woman.

Electricity sizzled in the air between them.

Releasing her, he climbed into his saddle and said, "Follow me."

They exited the stable and he took them north, past the well-worn trails used for guests. They rode along a dirt path that had been used by truck and hoof alike. On the left, a sliver of a mountain stream meandered almost parallel alongside the trail.

The path led toward stable number two. They skirted around the mountains, staying between the ivory-coated peaks. Mav pointed out elk and mule deer they spotted on the way. He stopped as Bianca took pictures with her phone.

"Planning on painting it?" he asked, more interested in who she was and what she liked, beyond simply the drive to get her naked.

"Most likely, now that I'm painting again. They're like nothing I've ever seen before. And I've visited the Highlands of Scotland and skied the Swiss Alps. But these are just breathtaking."

"So you like our mountains?"

"Yes, more than I imagined I would." She shot him a warm glance and looked away, but not before he spied the need in her gaze.

Her blatant desire for him made him want to pull her off the saddle and do very bad, wicked things with her.

When she'd finished taking pictures, he clicked his heels against Jack's flank, and they were off once more. Jack had an idea of where they were heading—since they had been there plenty—as they followed the stream. The path forked, with one trail heading toward the stables, but they took the left one that continued beside the stream.

He knew the moment they crossed the boundary. It must be something to do with the fact that it belonged to him. And he wasn't sure why he was bringing her on this path and to this place. They trotted up a slight incline through a bank of evergreens.

And then the view opened as they crested the ridge—the mountain field was a plateau that overlooked the stream. The three-sixty view was all mountains.

Bianca gasped. "It's incredible. I didn't realize the ranch went this far back, either."

"It doesn't," he replied, pleased by her response. She had her phone in her hand, snapping photos.

"Are we in the National Forest then?" she asked, stopping her picture taking for a moment and glancing his way.

"No. It's mine," he explained, studying her reaction.

"Yours? As in your land?"

He nodded. "Yep, all thirty-six acres."

"Maverick, it's a beautiful spot. I can see why you picked it. And are you planning to live here?" she asked.

"Yep. Eventually, once I get my place built. We're standing in what will likely be part of the house one day. There will be a barn and stables as well. It will be a longer trek to work, but it will be nice looking out my kitchen window at what belongs to me."

"It must be pretty satisfying. I don't have anything that belongs to me—not really, anyway. It's all family dwellings, even my flat in London. And I know that sounded dreadfully self-pitiful." She looked like she was going to say more but instead dismounted from Sunshine and walked away to peer over the ledge to the small stream.

Maverick swung off Jack's saddle and joined Bianca near the stream. "It sounds to me like it makes you unhappy."

"You don't know the half of it," she replied with such desolation, it gave him pause. It made him think of the day he had come upon her on the stairs when she had looked like her world had ended. He secured the horses, letting them graze on the nearby grass.

"Tell me." He approached, noticing tension had entered her slight frame.

"In my family, there are lots of expectations one must ascribe to in order to uphold the family name in polite society. It's ghastly, pretentious, and something I've never been able to master. As far as my mother is concerned, I am a total disappointment in every way that matters. My father isn't much better, as he tends to follow wherever my mum instructs him to proceed."

What it sounded was lonely. And it reminded him just how looks could be deceiving. When he had first met her and helped get her suitcases into her cabin, he had made a number of assumptions about her. Every single one of them had been wrong.

She glanced his way with a somber expression. "What about your family?"

Wasn't that a loaded fucking question? His family was the epitome of dysfunctional. "Nothing much to talk about. My dad knocked my mother up. They got married but were never happy with each other. They did it because of me, since back then, it was what one did. Although there wasn't anything resembling love between them. I split when I was eighteen; worked on different ranches for years, learning everything I could about wrangling, and landed here ten years ago. Dad died four years ago—drove drunk one night, and plowed into a tree. Mom still lives in the same house in Wyoming, but her sister lives with her now. We were never a close family. When my dad died, it had been two years since we had spoken." It was more like the three of them had been hostages, all living together until each one could make a break for it. Some days, Mav wondered if his dad had aimed for that tree.

"We make quite the pair, don't we? Families are so complicated." She didn't offer kind words or apologies or try to make him look for something redeemable about his upbringing. And it left him scrutinizing her and discovering a kindred spirit in the most unlikely person.

"But yours drove you to another country," he teased, without a lot of heat behind his words.

She snorted. "They did, for which I'm eternally grateful. I was suffocating. Being smothered daily by my mother's well-intentioned plans for my life. I'd almost forgotten that it was mine to live. If I would have stayed, I think my soul would have died."

He understood all too well about doing what one needed to survive. And that there was more than one kind of starvation. Her words brought his instincts to protect and shield her to the forefront. "And you're going to go back?"

"Yes. No... maybe. Shit, I haven't the foggiest clue. I'm still trying to figure out what I want, let alone what to do with myself." She gestured, frustration laced in every word.

"Why do you have to even consider going back if it makes you miserable? You could always stay here." Once the words left his mouth, he felt the tide of emotions he had kept hidden from himself up to this point surge to the fore. He wanted her to stay, as remarkable as that might seem. Because he had feelings for her. He didn't know how deep they ran but they were there. And they were something that they could explore, should she stay.

She laughed. "Wouldn't that be something? Me, living in the American Wild West. I do have an affinity for the land."

"Is it really that big of a stretch?" he asked, fishing to see if there was even the slightest chance he could convince her to stay.

"If you knew what I come from..." She shook her head with defeat clouding her gaze.

Maverick lost his cool. "That's a load of horse shit. Just because your parents want something different for you doesn't mean you need to toe the line they've laid out for you. If living in London makes you unhappy then what's the point in going back? And don't give me the *I have responsibilities* excuse."

She considered him. "Maybe you're right. It's something to think about, anyway."

"I bet I could convince you, princess." He tugged her close.

"Is that a fact?" she asked in a breathy voice. Her hands slid over his chest and felt like hot brands. Lust plowed his system.

"Yep." As he cupped her face in his hands, she stared at him with simmering need. Keeping his gaze on her, he lowered his mouth and kissed her. She sighed into his embrace. Her hands curled against his chest, creating little half-moons with her nails.

This woman ignited every cylinder in him to nuclear levels. She made him ache to be inside her. He deepened his kiss, caressed his way down her supple back to her fucking killer ass. He pulled her against him, letting her feel how much he desired her. His dick strained against the confines of his jeans, throbbing in need to feel the potent vise of her cunt.

He drank down her startled moan. His hands slid under her top and over the smooth skin of her lower back.

He trailed kisses down her neck.

"Maverick," she murmured huskily, the need prominent in her voice.

"Are you wet for me?" He nipped her neck where it met her shoulder.

"Yes."

"Show me," he demanded, and lifted his head.

She contemplated him, hesitating for a moment, before she undid the button and zipper on her jeans. She took one of his hands and moved it beneath the silk covering her pussy.

He dipped his fingers between her slit and found her

drenched. He groaned, and circled her clit with his index finger.

She gripped his hand, unconsciously rocking her hips to move against his finger. He knew that he couldn't just tease her. He had to have her, come hell or high water. Delving deeper, he penetrated her pussy, thrusting his finger in and out.

Her free hand clutched at his shoulder as he finger-fucked her tight hole. Mewls slipped from her mouth and her gaze grew heavy lidded. He inserted a second finger; the sound of her gasps had his dick jerking in his denim.

He watched desire fill her gaze. Her moans echoed in the valley. But there was no one but him to hear them.

Her head fell back as he increased his speed, plunging his fingers in deep. He gave her no quarter, needing to send her flying. When she stiffened against him, her cunt squeezing and rippling around his fingers as she climaxed, her gaze went blind.

He bent down and claimed her mouth, hungry and needy for more.

Removing his hand from her cunt, he sucked the juices and groaned at her musky flavor. Maverick came close to tearing his plaid off in his haste to remove it. He laid it on the ground and pulled her down onto her hands and knees.

"Maverick?" she questioned.

"I need to fuck you."

She moaned and tilted her hips. Hooking his fingers around her jeans and panties, he yanked them down to her knees, leaving her ass bare. Kneeling behind her, he made short work of his pants, shoving them and his boxers down far enough to free his dick.

The pretty pink lips of her labia glistened with dew. He guided his length through her slit, rubbing the head back and forth, until he finally aligned his shaft at her slick opening.

Maverick gripped her hips to hold her steady, and plowed his cock inside her.

Her back bowed, and she moaned.

"You feel like hot fucking silk vising my dick," he groaned. Withdrawing until only the tip remained, he thrust deep.

Feeling her skin to skin, he reveled in the sensations of her pussy clenching him, trying to draw him deeper inside her warmth. He shuttled his length, pounding inside her. He wanted her with a need bordering on obsession. Her moans of pleasure spurred him on.

Leaning forward, he slid his hands up to cup her tits, kneading and massaging the globes as he pumped his hips.

"Maverick," she moaned, thrusting her hips back, lost in her ecstasy.

At the way she said his name, he turned downright primal. He wanted to imprint himself on her so that no matter where they ended up, she would remember this—and him. As much as he yearned for more for the first time in his life, he more than anyone understood just how unforgiving life could be.

And in this, he knew he excelled. Her cries of ecstasy were a drug in his system. He rocked harder, gliding deeper with each thrust. Holding her close, he gave her more than he had any woman before, imbuing her with every part of himself as he loved her.

He pressed her forward until she was lying flat on his shirt, and he pummeled her cunt. He gripped her neck, his face beside hers.

He snaked his other hand beneath her and stroked her

swollen clit as he pounded. Her moans increased as she began fluttering around his cock. He nipped her earlobe.

"I want you to come for me, princess," he demanded, and pinched her clit as he slammed home.

Her mouth dropped open on a wordless scream. Her hips bucked. Her pussy spasmed as he thrust. And it was those hard, fluttering clenches that rocketed him over the ledge.

"Fuck." He groaned as he came, his dick jolting and spilling his load inside her clutching heat.

He pumped inside her until every drop had emptied from his shaft. Then he turned her face and took her mouth, kissing her with all the swelling emotions he didn't want to examine. He knew that was cowardly on his part.

But he also couldn't deny that she mattered to him, more than any woman ever had. She kissed him back, as lost in him as he was in her. It was something. He lifted his mouth and stared at her, resting his forehead against hers. She lifted her gaze.

And he felt his heart fucking drop.

Not ready for anything remotely like discussing feelings, he withdrew from her body. Rising, he helped her up, dusting her off a bit as she fixed her jeans.

He yanked his pants up, then picked up his shirt and beat the dust from it best he could, before he put it on. He brushed his lips over her forehead before he picked up his hat, settled it on his head, and strode over to where the horses were patiently grazing.

"Maverick." Her voice drifted over the field.

He glanced back. Her face was still flushed from their heated lovemaking. "Yeah?"

"Thanks for bringing me here. I like your place."

"Anytime, princess." He winked, trying to keep things light and maintain some semblance of distance.

But inside, everything within his chest warmed and expanded. The strange thing was that he could see her here. Not just as she was now, or had been as he screwed her brains out. But as it could be, coming home after a long day, and finding her here, waiting for him to return home.

Home and hearth were something he had always wanted for himself, but he'd never imagined the possibility he might want to share it. And Bianca was the last person he would have considered, but somehow, she was the only one he could picture here with him.

He didn't tell her that, of course, as he helped her mount Sunshine and leapt on Black Jack's saddle, or on their return ride to Silver Springs Ranch stables. Yet no matter how much he tried, he couldn't expel the vision from his mind.

15

*W*hen she waltzed into her cabin after both of her rides, Bianca's body was sore, but in all the right ways. Instead of a shower, she took a long soak in the tub, even adding Epsom salts to soothe her muscles. It had been years since she had ridden a horse for more than an hour. When she had done dressage and show jumping, she'd sit atop Moonbeam for hours on end, practicing until they were both exhausted.

Moonbeam was the Shagya Arabian her parents had gifted Bianca when she was eight and learning to ride. She'd loved that horse. She had been Bianca's best friend growing up. Whenever the stress and anxiety got too much for her, she would head to their stables to see Moonbeam, and take a ride. There had been nights when she had snuck out of the house while her parents were sleeping, gone to the stables, and spent the night curled up against Moonbeam so she could cry her tears in private.

And then her mother had sold Moonbeam while Bianca was away at her first semester of university. Bianca hadn't been given the courtesy of saying goodbye. It was something she had never forgiven her mother for, even after a decade had passed.

As soon as she had learned what her mother had done—over the Christmas holidays—Bianca had fought to discover who had purchased Moonbeam for the next eighteen months. Bianca had every intention of buying her back with some of her inheritance. Eventually, her father had caved and provided her with the name of the buyer.

But she was a month too late. Moonbeam had shattered her foreleg on a jump with her new rider, and had been put down.

Moonbeam's death gutted Bianca.

She had loved that horse with everything inside her. And she hated that Moonbeam had likely died believing Bianca had abandoned her.

That discovery had spawned a gargantuan fight with her mother, and propelled Bianca into studying art abroad, in Rome. She did it without her parents' help during her last two years of university. She didn't talk to them the entire time she was in Rome. And she had even begun making plans to stay.

But she had been drawn back all the same when she'd finished university.

Being at the ranch, riding and painting again, discovering depths of pleasure at Maverick's hands, were all things she wanted to continue so badly, she could taste it. He had planted the seed, tempting her with the possibility of staying in the United States. She would have to apply for a Work Visa. There would be tasks, like setting up a bank account. She likely wouldn't stay in this cabin unless she was able to work out a better deal for an extended stay. If not, there certainly had to be places available for rent, maybe something with a skylight for her artwork.

And there was even the possibility of applying for citizenship, if she decided that she never wanted to go back to London.

Damn Maverick for dangling the carrot and insinuating they would be able to continue whatever this thing was between them, that they had yet to define. In all her life, she had never experienced this edge of violent, passionate lovemaking.

Without a doubt, it was the best sex she had ever had.

The moment Maverick touched her, her brain slipped right out of her head. It was uncanny. And hot, wickedly carnal, and at times, filthy—the way they tended to go at one another like animals.

Not to mention the difference without a condom.

That first time, she had been too hot to trot, aching, and past the point of comprehending anything beyond the pleasure overwhelming her system to truly notice or pay attention. But every time since then, she paid attention to the skin-on-skin contact. It was the most amazing feeling. She absolutely loved it—it was sexy and dangerous, but nothing in the world felt that good.

And it made her consider the man himself, given he had grown on her considerably since their inauspicious first meeting. Maverick was stubborn enough that he could give lessons in it. He was domineering, which, outside the bedroom, tended to make them clash. But in a bedroom-like setting, even if it happened to be outside, he assumed command of their lovemaking, and she didn't mind that at all. In fact, she craved it. She wondered what other depraved acts and limits he would propel her into because it suited him.

God, there were fantasies she had that, before meeting Maverick, she considered far too taboo for her to try. Even when the thought of them aroused her beyond measure. Maybe she should bring them up the next time he came by. Perhaps tonight, even.

What would he say if she told him that she had always wanted to try anal sex? He was a Dom. She knew about the lifestyle because of all the society people who were into kink. They looked strait-laced and pompous, but there was a subset that liked to get freaky and attend sex parties at country estates. A few of her girlfriends had mentioned their experiences—whispered discreetly, of course.

Bianca had told him more about herself than she had anyone in a long time. He'd been kind and understanding. And had opened up to her about his past.

He hadn't mentioned any siblings. His upbringing sounded cold, and heartbreaking. Where she had experienced loads of attention to an extreme bent, the opposite could be said about him. It made her want to weep for the child he had been, to have never known warmth. And yet, in spite of his start, he had carved out an incredible life for himself. He awed her with his depth of character and independence. It took someone with immense internal strength to survive such a desolate childhood and not grow bitter.

And he'd unknowingly voiced a wish that she hadn't even allowed herself to fully consider as a prospect. But floating the possibility of her staying—she wanted it, badly. The thought of never going back to those blasted rigid social functions, or no longer having to mind her words in case she caused her family to be ostracized for generations... there were no words for how incredible it made her feel.

Except hopeful.

Optimism rose within her chest, budding and growing, at the thought of having a place of her own in the tiny little town. Getting a chance to develop the burgeoning friendships with Amber and Grace.

And perhaps, if she was lucky, continue this relationship with Maverick—and what she considered the most surprising turn of events. If someone had told her, when she'd boarded her flight at Heathrow, that within two weeks of being in America, she would fall headlong into a passionate love affair with a rough around the edges, dominant cowboy, she would have laughed in their faces.

She didn't have love affairs.

Not since her mother had put a stop to her time in Italy, tearing her away from the man who had initiated her in the art of lovemaking. Renaud had been Bianca's art instructor —twenty years older, incredibly sexy—and had sensually awakened her to the pleasures of the flesh. His lovemaking had been sweet and intense. She had loved him with all the pent-up longing in her heart, but while he'd had great affection for her, it hadn't been love on his end. With her unschooled heart broken, she hadn't put up a fight when her mum arrived on her doorstep saying it was time she came home. In the years since, Bianca had been with a few men, but the relationships weren't serious, and the interactions had always left her disappointed.

None of them held a candle to sex with Maverick.

The man was fierce, passionate, and dominant. A simple look or touch from him made her burn for his wicked love.

After she exited her bath, she took time smoothing some lotion into her skin. Bianca figured Maverick would visit that night, and was primping like women had been doing for centuries to dazzle men they were involved with. It was a rite of passage, pampering her skin, ensuring it was soft and silky. While he hadn't explicitly asked or stated that he would see her later when they'd returned to the stables, it had been implied in the smoldering intensity in his eyes as he'd helped her dismount Sunshine.

He'd tenderly placed her on her feet, and her heart had rolled over in her chest, and exposed its soft underbelly.

She grimaced.

There were so many complications in her life. Like the pesky little detail that she was engaged to be married in a few short weeks—to another man. It made the relationship with Maverick wrong on so many levels. She hadn't told him she was engaged, either. Because she'd figured that first night with him would be the only time—a simple one-night stand that would be over once the sun came up. He was the exact opposite of the man her mother expected her to marry. There was nothing refined or genteel about Maverick.

Except now, that engagement—the secret she was holding—mocked her. If she planned on staying, it meant she would need to come clean to Maverick.

She had never considered that she would start falling for the rough and tumble cowboy. But she couldn't deny the joy surging inside her at the thought of him, or the way he made her feel.

She could hear her mother's voice asking her once more: *but what about Peter?*

What about him? Bianca hadn't heard from her *fiancé* at all since she'd left London. Why should she think about him or his feelings? He certainly wasn't considering hers at all. They were friends, but that was as deep as the relationship went.

And for the life of her, she couldn't picture Peter pulling her down onto the ground outdoors to make passionate love to her. Hell, all they had ever done was exchange a few tepid kisses.

But the wedding was what her mother wanted—to have her daughter married to the son of a duke.

Bianca wanted nothing to do with it. The thought of marrying Peter made her abjectly miserable. She had tried broaching the subject once; explained that she didn't want to marry Peter.

And her mother's response?

That Bianca needed to pull her act together. Their families had decided on this marriage when she'd been thirteen and Peter sixteen. It was a Peabody tradition that they arrange strategically advantageous unions for their children. Just as her father had been matched with her mother, so too had Bianca been paired with Peter. It was Bianca's duty to her family to uphold tradition, after all.

It was bloody archaic, was what it was.

And it was a barrier, keeping her from the life she wanted—to live simply, with heart and passion.

She was envious of her cowboy, because he knew his place in the world and where he fit in. While she had no idea where she belonged. All she knew was that it wasn't as Peter's wife.

Even if she caved and headed back to London when her time was up, she couldn't marry him. The repercussions would be swift and severe, and the majority would come from her mother.

She shoved the depressing thoughts away. Ignoring her problems was a trick she excelled at. Instead, she selected her undergarments with care, and Maverick in mind. Her cowboy sure seemed to love her taste in panties.

The thought of his low, rumbled groan when he'd

discovered the black lace and satin panties with the little bow in front made her sex clench.

Instead of painting—mainly because she was running low on a few necessary paint colors and would have to make a run into town tomorrow for more supplies—she sat on the couch with her sketch pad and phone. Bringing up the images she had snapped on her mobile, she turned them into charcoal drawings. She wanted to take some of them beyond the charcoal medium, and paint them. There were a few she even wanted to try as watercolors.

She might have to make some frames. There were a few that just demanded a larger canvas than what Archie's Art Supply offered in premade ones. Making frames entailed buying large sheets of canvas, selecting the wood she wanted to use, then measuring, sawing, and reforging the wood into a frame. She would have to get the wood for that, and would also need tools.

Perhaps Maverick could help her with that and could lend her some tools.

Her stomach growled, and she checked the time. It was well past the dinner hour, but she had got caught up.

The sun was setting as she microwaved her meal and poured herself a glass of wine. She hated that she was listening for the solid sound of his boots on her cabin stairs.

Oh, she had it bad for the cowboy.

When she'd finished her meal, she poured a second glass of wine. Bianca was determined not to pine if Maverick was a no show. They hadn't made any promises or plans. Ergo, she would focus on what she could control.

It was late enough that she changed into pajamas. She stripped, and threw on her short nightgown. The silky, pale blue material fell to midthigh, and was comfortable, while also having a hint of sex appeal. She donned her robe and trod back into the living room. She curled up on the couch with her wine, and a blanket covering her legs.

The thought of him had her reaching for her paper and pencil, and she began a new sketch of Maverick. The way he had looked atop the black stallion today—confident, strong, and master of his domain, with the glimmer of sensual heat in his gaze. His face and image dominated the page until she'd completed that portrait. She flipped the page, and started another one of him.

This one was from the other night in her studio—the cheeky look he had slanted her way right after she had added a streak of blue to his cheek. Those golden eyes had held the promise of retribution. She flipped to another page, drawing him again and again.

If she wasn't strong enough to grab what she wanted and tell her mother to get bent, at least she would have these to remember him by. The thought of leaving made her chest ache. It was far different than the thought she'd had when she'd left London to travel here. Freedom had infused her then, along with hefty doses of fear and anxiety.

But she would miss Maverick. He was important, if for no other reason than he had shown her another way of existing.

As the night deepened, she grew knackered and rested her head against her hand, staring at the completed image on her lap. It was the way his face had looked while taking her against the vanity in the bathroom.

The second glass of wine might have been a bad idea. Her eyelids slid shut. She would rest them for a minute.

Bianca was out cold, with the sketchbook resting in her lap.

*T*hud, *thud, thud.*

Bianca jolted awake. The movement sent the pencil still dangling in her hand flying. It landed on the hardwood floor and rolled beneath the coffee table. The pounding thumps on the front door continued.

Groggy and disoriented, she tossed the sketchpad onto the coffee table and headed for the door.

"Just a bloody minute." She yanked it open, ready to give the person on the other side a blistering lecture.

It died on her tongue.

He was so fucking handsome, he made her ache.

Maverick had his palms braced upon the door frame. An intense sensual expression that carried a hint of danger shrouded his features, and he looked like carnal sin in his black plaid and denim. He still hadn't shaved. The dark shadow beard had her stomach clenching. Delicious tingles shivered along her spine. She adored the rough scrape of it against her inner thighs when he was going down on her—really, anywhere his mouth moved and it grazed her skin.

In the short time they had been making bad decisions,

he had shown her parts of herself, things she never would have imagined she enjoyed in the bedroom, that she loved.

Narrowing her gaze, she glanced more closely. "Are you drunk? Have one too many beers tonight, Ace?"

"Not even a little," he said, nudging his way inside with his big body and shutting the door with a resounding thud. He prowled into her space. His nimble fingers unbuttoned his plaid, the lascivious intent crystal clear in his eyes.

Everything inside her body coiled tight.

In this moment, he resembled a mountain lion stalking a deer, making their movements a dance of predator and prey. Either she stayed standing still and let him catch her, or she could retreat.

Bianca chose withdrawal even though she understood with perfect clarity he would not relent. Truthfully, she was thrilled he was here. His dark, dangerous desire left her breathless.

Was it getting hot in the cabin, or was it merely her body going up in flames as he pursued her with wicked intent?

He trailed her movements, removing his shirt and exposing his ripcord chest. She loved his chest—all the rangy, ropy muscles without an inch of give. He was strong and firm, without being too bulked up.

Bianca shifted from sleepy to heightened awareness and pulsating need. Her breath caught in her lungs. She trembled as he stalked her.

Maverick backed her up against the couch backrest and bracketed her body with his arms. Pressing his advantage, using his larger form, he crowded her against the leather until there wasn't a sliver of space between them.

Heat curled inside her. Her sex throbbed at his nearness. She hated the power he had over her. But there was no denying he made her feel every pinprick of pleasure—every point where their bodies were aligned, smoldered.

"You smell like a cesspit." She wrinkled her nose as she caught the whiff of smoke and liquor.

He removed his hat and tossed it onto the side table, never taking his eyes off her. His hands—those big, strong, callous-roughened hands—caressed up and down the sides of her body. "A buddy needed a wingman tonight at the local watering hole."

"So you just went for support and not to pick up a woman yourself?" she asked, and it came out much more snidely than she would have preferred. She would rather he was unaware of how the thought of him with other women made her feel—jealous, with a huge dash of insecurity.

He cupped her chin, threaded his fingers through her hair, and tilted her face up at an angle. "See, that's it, right there. It's rather masochistic but that uppity, condescending tone of yours gets me rock hard every fucking time."

"I happen to speak proper English; there's nothing condescending about it. It's fine by me if this thing between us, our bad decision making, is over. We have no claims on the other. We've not made promises or declared exclusivity or undying love."

"You want a pledge from me? I vow, by the time I've finished fucking you tonight, your voice will be hoarse from all your screams of ecstasy."

A delicious shiver of anticipation zinged along her spine and pooled in her sex. The cowboy was undeniably potent, especially when he talked dirty like that. She had never figured that she was a woman who liked dirty talk during sex, and boy, had he proven her wrong. When it came out of his mouth, she bloody adored it. "Be that as it may, I don't expect promises from you. I understand perfectly that this is merely a sexual fling without any parameters."

"And what if I wanted to keep you? Wanted this to be exclusive, and to train you in the art of submission?" he murmured, his tone deadly serious as he studied her.

"We're total opposites. We don't even like each other," she protested feebly. Because inside, she was dancing a jig. Happiness soared through her. He wanted to keep her. And more kinky sex with him? Yes, please.

He pressed his hips hard against her pelvis, letting her feel every solid inch of his desire. In a low bedroom voice that rumbled from his chest into hers and added to the quixotic potency of her need, he said, "Oh, we like each other fine, princess. In fact, let me show you just how much I like you."

Maverick slid to his knees, keeping that intense, dark gold gaze trained on her. His hands caressed her hips through the fabric. She bit her bottom lip as his palms slid further down, below the hem of her nightgown to the naked flesh of her thighs. The rough pads of his stroking fingertips left a fiery trail in their wake.

He gripped her left leg. He lifted it up and rested her knee over his broad shoulder, letting her calf dangle against his back.

The move shifted the hem of her robe and nightgown, exposing her intimate flesh. With a rough, male groan, he leaned in and pressed an open-mouthed kiss against her covered mound.

He liked her panties.

But the silky barrier proved to be too much of an obstacle for him to reach his prime directive. He grasped the thin straps on her hips. With a single, hard yank, he ripped the offending garment off.

"Oh," Bianca gasped.

Moisture flooded her sex and her hips jerked. Her nipples stabbed against her nightgown. The cowboy was controlled aggression. His eyes were suffused with dark lust. And his desire ignited a maelstrom of need pounding in her veins. It was in every ragged breath, in every beat of her heart. Blood rushed in her ears.

"Remove your nightgown. I want you to play with your tits while I eat your pretty cunt," he commanded in a firm tone.

Holy god!

Heat slammed into her.

Dominance rolled off him in undiluted waves. She shuddered at the need battering her. And he had barely touched her. Would she survive his sinful desire without going up in flames?

Her fingers trembled as she undid the sash of her robe and let the material fall, sliding down off her arms and falling over the backrest. Tugging the hem of her nightgown, she raised it slowly, like she was unveiling her form inch by inch. A secretive thrill blared through her as his gaze darkened as she revealed herself.

His hungry stare told her how much he adored her body.

She drew the material over her head and tossed it behind her, not caring where it landed. Her entire focus dwindled to the half-dressed man kneeling between her spread thighs.

His fingers parted her soaking wet folds with his thumbs. Cool air hit her sex and teased a moan from her lips.

"Play with your tits." He growled the command, waiting for her to comply. Making it clear he wouldn't begin his wicked assault on her sex until she followed his orders.

Bianca was filled with the desire to please him and submit to his dark demands.

With that aim in mind, yearning to experience his wicked mouth on her sex, she deliberately drew her hands up her torso, moving her palms achingly slowly, up past her belly and over her ribcage, until she reached the sensitive globes and cupped them.

The moment she obeyed, kneading and massaging her breasts, his hot gaze trained on her movements, his tongue shot out and lashed her clit.

She sucked in a breath. Fierce pleasure overwhelmed her system. Bianca's gaze grew heavy lidded. He fluttered his tongue over her flesh. She moaned. It had never been this good before him. She'd had lovers give her oral, yet never in her wildest imaginings did she think it could feel like this. She trembled with the force of pleasure infusing her being, and plucked at her stiff nipples. She had never touched herself like this in front of anyone before, and it only added more flames to the inferno, cranking the heat wattage up a thousand degrees.

Maverick laved and lapped at her pussy. Every caress sent lightning strikes of pleasure shooting from her clit to her sex, and bliss built in ceaseless waves. The mewls spilling from her lips were unintelligible. She was close—so very close to an earth-shattering pinnacle that she canted her hips against his mouth, needing more friction and pressure, reaching for the climax just out of her grasp.

But Maverick growled, his gaze narrowed. He clamped her hips, stalling movements of any kind.

She protested. "Sir, please."

Yet her plea fell on deaf ears. He held her hips tight,

keeping her from attaining what she wanted. She was seconds from disobeying him and following her id that wanted satiation now.

Maverick thrust his tongue in her sheath, fucking her with it.

"Oh god." She tossed her head back, the leg holding her body up trembling with the pleasure flooding through her. His tongue stroked deep in a furious pace. Circling her swollen clit, his fingers rubbed and flicked back and forth against her nub. She gripped her breasts tight as her body charged toward bliss.

The man was determined to deliver on his promise.

"Oh god," she cried as he nipped at her flesh and thrust two digits inside. The pumping glide of his fingers fucking her stoked the inferno to blistering heights. Her moans echoed in the cabin, loud enough that anyone walking by would hear them. And she didn't know why but the thought of other people hearing them, knowing they were having sex, was a huge turn-on.

Bianca came. Her body coiled tight and imploded. Her hips bucked and she wailed, "Maverick."

Quaking from the overwhelming force, the leg holding her up gave, and she fell. But she never hit the floor. Maverick caught her. In all her life, she had never felt this safe and protected. He rose to his feet, hoisted her up, and wrapped her legs around his waist.

Those big hands cupped her bottom and squeezed. "I've got you."

Yes, he did, in more than one way. What would he say if she told him she wanted to keep him too?

17

Bianca threaded her arms around Mav's neck. Carrying her, he strode to the bedroom. She pressed her lips against his throat, roving over his skin, placing light kisses. She loved the taste of him in her mouth. Nipping his earlobe, pleasure shot through her at his male groan.

Maverick laid her gently on the bed. It wasn't lost on her that he still hadn't removed his jeans. And she could see the outline of his erection pressing against the denim. Her fingers itched to touch him. The other day, when she had given him head, he had denied her the chance to have him come in her mouth. And she wanted it so badly, her mouth watered at the thought.

He unbuckled his belt. "Give me your hands."

"Wait, I want—"

"That's not how this works, princess. Unless you want me to stop completely?"

With a frustrated sigh, she said, "No. I don't want that, but I do want your cock in my mouth."

His gazed turned molten. "Well now, I think I can make that happen. But we're going to do it with a little bondage."

Victory shivered through her. "I'd like that. It's one of my fantasies."

"Which one? Being bound while you're fucked, or having my cock in your mouth?"

"Both." She whispered the admission raggedly.

"Fuck." His hot gaze scorched her. "I never imagined under all that primness, was a filthy submissive with passion to rival my own. You're such a surprise, princess."

Her pussy throbbed at his words. It was the truth. She thrilled at all the depraved, naughty sex. She craved his domination.

"Any other fantasies I should know about?" He disrobed, removing his boots first, before attacking his pants. She watched him draw his jeans and boxers down his legs. She licked her lips. Naked, his cock jutted proudly from his pelvis.

She blushed at his demand that she expose herself further, but was unable to look away.

"Tell me, or as punishment, I will deny you further orgasms tonight. I'm good at doing that too. I will even make you watch me jerk off and come all over your tits."

Lust punched through her.

By the set of his jaw, he would carry out his threat too. She huffed and debated until his hand circled his staff, slowly stroking it from root to tip, and back down again. "I've sort of always wanted to try anal, and that other thing you just said. Really, I think I would be open to a lot that I've just never had the chance or the partner to experience it with."

It was as close to an admission of her feelings as she was

comfortable with presently. He was already laying her open and making her divulge all her secrets—save one.

She watched the play of light on his face as her fantasy and words registered. A slow, carnal smile slid across his face. "I can help you with those, princess. Have any lube around?"

She sighed. "No."

"Another time on the anal then. But the others... I'd love to come on your tits. Hell, I want to fuck them." Maverick joined her on the mattress and lay back, putting his hands behind his head. "I'm all yours, princess."

Heat lanced through her at being given carte blanche access to his body. Rising, she straddled his legs. Sliding her hand around the base of his shaft, she was rewarded with his dark hiss. She stroked him, imitating the way he had fondled his cock. But her focus dipped from his face to his member.

Leaning forward, she licked him from root to tip, flattening her tongue over the crest and circling the ridge. His salty musk flavor hit her tongue. She teased him, running her tongue over the thick veins, marveling at how soft his skin was there, and just how firm.

She shot her gaze up his body and connected with his dark gaze. Opening her mouth, she enveloped the head and drew him inside.

"Fuck," Maverick groaned in dark delight.

It was all the encouragement she needed to continue sucking him. She hollowed her cheeks and took as much of his shaft inside as possible. But he was just huge—even deep throating, she wouldn't be able to fit him all in. She added her hand as she moved her mouth up and down his cock.

She wanted him to come inside her mouth. Wanted to feel the hot splash as he spurted and lost himself in ecstasy because of what she did with her lips and tongue. She bobbed her head and sucked him hard.

His hips rocked beneath her, thrusting his shaft inside her mouth. He was controlled—at first. But as she gave him head, that control slipped. His hands gripped the sides of her head as he began to fuck her throat.

She loved every depraved second of it, humming and moaning around his dick, coating it with her saliva. Moisture seeped from her pussy.

"Enough," he growled, and went to lift her off him.

She beseeched him. "Please, Sir, I want you to come in my mouth."

"Is this another one of your fantasies?"

"Yes." There were so many. And more seemed to present themselves each time she was with him.

He looked up at the ceiling, his chest rising and falling rapidly, before he met her gaze once more and said, "I want you to swallow every drop. Don't miss one, or I will have to spank you."

She moaned, but didn't waste time. She took him back in her mouth, watching his face for signs of his impending climax. His hands cupped her head as he rocked his hips. His pace increased, and she reveled in the pleasure she was giving him.

His groans and hisses filled the bedroom. His cock swelled as she sucked him again and again.

His dick jolted. "Oh fuck, I'm coming."

Hot liquid filled her mouth as his orgasm wracked his big body. She tried to get it all, really she did.

"That's it, princess. Swallow every drop." He thrust again and again as he came.

Bianca lifted her head regretfully and sat back on her heels, breathing heavily. She was so turned on, a few swipes against her clit and she would go off like a rocket. But she had also failed.

"I'm sorry. I missed some."

Maverick hauled her up his body and crushed his mouth over hers. She clung to him. He conquered her with his hot, greedy lips, drinking down her moans. He tore his mouth from hers. "Twenty good swats ought to do it."

"But I said I was sorry!" she sputtered as he flipped her over until she was face down on the mattress with her bare ass over his legs.

"And after this, you will work harder to follow my instructions."

He didn't give her any time to prep before the first swat landed with a loud thwack. Her eyes widened. It was more surprising than painful. But the first few spanks were just a warm up.

By the fifth and sixth hard crack, her butt burned, and she was biting back her yelps. And yet, as she worked to breathe through the pain, it transformed into the most acute ecstasy. Instead of shying away from the spanking, she was tilting her hips up and begging him for more.

Maverick massaged the burning globes. "This is unexpected. I never imagined you'd get hot for discipline but I stand corrected. Your pussy's soaking wet, princess."

She moaned at his naughty words—too far gone, her throat thick with pleasure.

He shifted her body and rolled them until she was lying on her back. It made the burning agony in her bum climb even higher.

With his knee, he nudged her thighs open and settled his body between hers. His mouth claimed hers. She whimpered and writhed against him. He caught her hands in his and lifted them above her head. Before she could realize his intent, he used the belt he had looped around a wooden slat in the headboard to tie her wrists together.

She moaned as he lifted his mouth and checked the bindings.

Then he shot her a carnal stare, and the corners of his lips curled as he shifted. He leaned down and sucked a ripe nipple into the hot cavern of his mouth. And with her hands bound, there was nothing she could do to stop him. Lava poured through her veins.

God, did Maverick love her boobs. Those big, rough hands pushed and smooshed them together. Then he shifted back and forth between the globes. His skilled tongue teased the stiff peaks, lashing and flicking them, only to then envelop them into his mouth where he sucked deeply upon them.

"Maverick," she pleaded, writhing as her desire built. She had already been near climax from the blow job and then the spanking, but now she ached for release.

He released her nipple with a smacking sound. "What did I tell you? I plan on making you climax multiple times tonight. We've barely begun, princess. This won't be over quickly, and you will come when I allow it."

He squeezed a nipple harshly between his fingers. Plea-sure-pain sliced through her from her breast straight to her pussy. She issued a throaty moan. There was pain present, but it combined with the pleasure, which made it epic. It shouldn't be something she liked but god, she did.

"I think you'd enjoy clamps. Next time, I need to remember to bring my goodie bag, or get you to my cabin and take you in my bed. That way we can try some clamps and see how you do with a butt plug."

Her pussy fluttered at the image his words created, and she moaned.

He chuckled darkly. "Someone likes the thought of that. Tell me, ever have a man slap your tits or take a flogger to them?"

She shook her head. "No."

But weirdly enough, the thought of having him do it, made her feel like her body had been shoved in an over-heated oven.

"But you like it when I spank you?"

"Yes, Sir." She did. She had not just liked it but had loved every naughty second of it.

"I'm going to try that with your tits. If you don't like it, use the safeword *red,* and I will stop."

"Okay." She was just on the side of pleasure where everything he did heightened her bliss.

He lifted up, holding himself up with one arm. He drew back and swatted her boob. Pain shot through her that quickly morphed into pleasure. He repeated the whack a second and a third time. The rough slap ricocheted plea-sure-pain from her nipple down to her clit, which throbbed.

"Oh god," she moaned, arching her back, greedy for more.

He shot her a devilish grin. "See? I had a feeling you'd like it, princess."

He continued smacking her breasts, first one globe and then the other, back and forth. He increased the intensity and force behind each one until they were an angry red, and throbbing. She writhed. Flames licked over her skin, burning away all pretenses of who she was as she became someone new under his passionate tutelage, and was slowly being incinerated in ecstasy.

Her stiff nipples ached at the touch. He stopped the kinky torture, kneading the abused mounds. The gnawing burn throbbed with his tongue swiping over the peaks. She arched at the lightning bolts of electricity that shot directly down to her pussy.

Maverick traveled south, nipping, and marking her flesh as he went, until his face hovered back over her pussy. His nostrils flared and his gaze darkened with lust. "Your cunt is fucking drenched."

"But I need—"

"I told you, this is going to take a long time tonight. Settle back and enjoy my mouth on you, because I have every intention of drawing the pleasure out as long as possible tonight. Until you are screaming and begging me to fuck you. Until then, let me hear those breathy moans and little sounds you make."

With his gaze on her face, he lowered his mouth and latched it around her clit. Pleasure flash fried her system. He lashed and laved her sex. Curled his tongue around the swollen nub. Applied fingers and teeth to his erotic assault. Until she was mindless with need and undulating against his torrid assault. She whimpered and strained against the leather belt restraining her. He bit down on her clit, and thrust two fingers inside her. She splintered.

"Oh god!" Bianca came. Hard.

Her hips jerked. Her legs shook. Her pussy clenched and shuddered. And still he lapped at her cream like he was addicted and had no intention of giving her what she really wanted—which was him banging her brains out. Every facet of her being narrowed down to the oral stimulation. She entered a bliss-infused haze, where even the air moving over her skin added to her pleasure. He sent her flying again and again, until her pussy ached to feel him in her swollen tissues. She rocked her pelvis, craving more, craving everything.

"Maverick, please fuck me," she whimpered, writhing.

He lifted his head from her mound. Finally.

His stubble-covered chin was coated with her cream. He licked his lips, like he didn't want to miss a single drop of it. She groaned at the naughty decadence of the act.

He rose onto his knees. His stiff cock jutted as he positioned his large body between her thighs.

Maverick held his dick in one hand and swiped the head through her swollen cleft. She whimpered and rocked her hips. He pressed his palm against her hip bone, holding her steady as he lined his shaft up with her entrance.

As he inserted just the tip, his gaze flicked to her face. When their gazes connected, he plunged deep inside her sheath in a single thrust. Her back arched at the ecstasy, at the bliss bombarding her system as he stretched her channel. She strained against the leather holding her hands prisoner.

On his knees, he held her thighs and pumped his shaft in long, smooth strokes. He was controlled with his thrusts. Her mouth remained open from a string of moans. The breathy, high-pitched sounds filled the room. And she knew without a doubt that she could fall for him. Do that long, graceful swan dive plunge. There was a sliver of worry that she already *had* fallen.

But then he ratcheted her desire up even higher, thrusting in fast, pounding digs that left her breathless.

"I need to touch you," she cried, undulating and writhing as her body drew in tight.

"Hold on just a little longer, princess." He pummeled her cunt.

He reared a hand back and struck the hood of her clit, right as he slammed his cock inside, balls deep.

"Oh," she keened. The orgasm almost made her levitate off the bed. She bucked and screamed as she came, her climax like a battering ram to her system as she trembled and quaked around his thrusting shaft.

Maverick leaned forward, still deeply entrenched in her pussy, and released her wrists. He drew them down to her sides, modifying his position so that their torsos were aligned. Propping himself up on his elbows, he took her mouth as he moved, rocking, and plunging in time with his tongue thrusting in her mouth.

Her hands gripped him, sliding to his back and holding on. She returned his kiss with all the passion and emotions he engendered in her. Never in a million years had she believed she would have a sex life, one that was filled with passion—and possibly more than she thought was feasible.

The possibilities of what they could be, stretched before her. And she clung to him, moving, thrusting her hips, taking him deep inside her body, and even inside her heart—only to discover he was already there. Taking up space. Dominating it, and her, until he was all she could see.

His tempo increased. His thrusts grew more frantic and hurried. He tore his mouth from hers.

"Look at me," he demanded.

Bianca lifted her heavy lids until their gazes collided. His liquid gold eyes simmered. If she was being fanciful, she would say that she saw her future in his eyes. One in a cabin much like this, along a pretty mountain stream, where she painted while he was at work and waited for him to return each evening, to hold her and love her, to make babies with her.

It was all there, she just had to be brave and take what she wanted. Uncertainty kept her from reaching out, from declaring herself. But that didn't mean those feelings, hopes and wishes weren't there.

Because they were, and as much as she yearned for them, they terrified her.

All her life, the things she had desired most had always been taken from her. So even as he loved her, she knew fear. Fear that the parts of herself he had helped her unveil would be wrenched from her.

Maverick's control snapped, as if the tether leashing his control had broken in two. She dug her nails into his back, clawing at him as his pace crescendoed and he hammered his cock inside her.

His grunts joined her moans and the wet slap of flesh. He pistoned in her channel and buried his face in her neck as he gathered her close. Both of them were lost in their pleasure, reaching as they undulated and thrust, hips meeting again and again as they raced for the shining peak together.

Her body detonated. There was no other word for it. Her climax struck. She wailed as she quaked and trembled. He stiffened against her, and his low groan as he followed her over the ledge had more flutters and aftershocks erupting inside her.

They rocked until every wave receded, and all that remained were the staccato beats of their hearts as they floated in bliss.

Maverick lifted his head and said, "See, and that was just the first round. Give me fifteen minutes before we start the next one."

"We'll kill each other."

"Ah, but what a way to go, princess. Besides, I don't think I could go longer without being inside you again. I have this need in me for you."

She inhaled a shaky breath. It was as close to an admission of his feelings as he seemed able to make. It was more than enough, for now. She laid her palm on his face. "I'm glad you stopped by tonight. Because I've developed the same need."

The corners of his lips curled up and he grinned, shifting his hips. And then she gasped as he lengthened and hardened inside her.

"I'm not going to need those fifteen minutes after all," he murmured.

She groaned as he proceeded to show her how just many times they could love one another throughout the long night. It was one of the best nights of her life.

18

It was the damndest thing.

Maverick ran a brush over Rosie, taking care of the sweet mare after her morning slate of rides. But his mind was miles away, focused on the previous night as it replayed over and over again.

Bianca's cabin was situated right on the corner where the road split—one way headed toward more guest cabins, and the other leading directly to his house. On his way back from the bar, he'd had every intention of avoiding her and going straight home. They had already had sex on his property, quenching his need. On his entire drive back to the ranch, he kept listing reasons for bypassing her cabin.

They had already had sex that day. Their relationship was growing too intense. He didn't do long term relationships or commitments, and yet when they had been on his property, he'd pushed for her to stay in Colorado.

With that all in mind, he'd figured they needed some space and distance. Avoiding interactions and her place was the best way to sever ties and nip his addiction to her in the bud before it got much worse.

Which was why when Tanner had asked Mav to accompany him to the bar, he'd figured it was the best course of action. There was a group of coeds staying at the ranch who Tanner planned on meeting up with, and there were plenty to go around. So he'd gone because of this fascination he had for Bianca. He needed to shift to another woman and break the hold she had over him.

He knew the timing of the outing after their trail ride yesterday was bad, and made him seem like the stereotypical playboy. But he was spooked at the feelings inside him. He didn't do attachments with women.

He'd sat at the bar while Tanner charmed the coeds, some of whom had preened and batted their lashes in Mav's direction, giving him an open invitation. He could have gone back with any one of them for a fun night. Hell, it was something he and Tanner had done on more than one occasion. Before Bianca's advent into his life, it was exactly what he would have done.

But did he?

Nope.

And why was that?

Because he wanted the woman who drove him crazy and made him burn with illicit desire. She was in his fucking blood. He didn't much care for it. Nor did he have any idea what the fuck he was supposed to do with it.

So he stewed. Tried to figure out a way around the connection.

But like a man possessed, when her cabin came into view, with the lights still on, he'd veered off course. Because the honorable thing to do would be to tell her in person that this thing between them wasn't working for him any longer.

Except when she'd answered the door in her sleepy, rumpled state, her pale blue silk robe slipping down, exposing a slim shoulder and the spaghetti strap of her nightgown, he had lost his damn head. Potent need had slammed through him, flash fried all his circuits. Sweet Jesus, but he had taken one look in her sleepy goddess eyes and needed to take her, make her scream in ecstasy. He'd taken her, availed himself of her killer form again and again with relish, until she was all he could see. Until his flesh carried her scent, and his mouth was full of her flavor. Until his dick grew sore and would no longer rise thanks to over use.

He stayed the night with her body wrapped around his, more at peace than he could recall.

In a short time, he had developed a case for Bianca, one he couldn't seem to shake. Mav, the man who never took the same woman to bed twice. Suddenly, he couldn't get enough of just one.

It was a startling and rather dismaying revelation.

He was thoroughly enamored. It was as if she had bewitched him. Bianca was a combination of fire and ice. Those flames riveted him. When he touched her, she shifted from snooty disdain to blazing inferno, clutching him like he was the freaking god of sex.

And the fantasies she'd admitted last night. Fuck.

He had no clue what to do about her or how to proceed, moving forward. Not when he was having thoughts of claiming and keeping her.

Hell, he had posed the question. Admitted that he wanted to keep her. Proving that, while they might not always get along outside of the bedroom, in it, they were perfectly in sync.

He kept spending the night with her. Enjoyed the feel of her body cuddled against him.

It left his emotions in a complete tumult. Because what was he going to do if he couldn't convince her to stay?

This morning, after a quick bout of sex before he left her place, she'd mentioned he shouldn't expect her at the stables today. She had errands to run in town instead. But hell, he was going to miss seeing her in those skintight jeans, and watching her ride Sunshine while imagining her riding him.

God, what she did to him, the little moans she made when he was buried deep inside her.

"He's got it bad, y'all," Emmett said from just outside the stall Maverick was in.

Mav shot his friend a cross glance. Emmett's gray plaid shirt was coated with dust. Tanner and Noah were with him. The trio had shit-eating grins stamped across their features. Of the bunch, Noah was the only one who looked remotely respectable, but then he wasn't normally out on the trail or range each day.

"See, I told ya. He's brooding," Noah said, a lopsided smile on his face.

Mav wasn't brooding. He was evaluating the circumstances in order to make the best decision for both parties moving forward. He cast a deadpan glare at his friends, unwilling to give them any fodder. "What the hell are you morons jabbering on about?"

"Only that you're neck deep in it with the British chick." Tanner chuckled, mirth shrouding his visage.

Fear clamped around Mav's chest and squeezed. He denied it. "No. I'm not. We're enjoying each other while she's in the country. That's all."

Even so, a voice inside mocked him for denying the obvious. From the start, the first night, their interaction had been way more than simple, sexy fun. He craved her and their off the charts chemistry. Each time he assuaged the desperate ache inside, the moment they were done, he wanted her again.

"Denial is one of the stages. Just ask the Doc on that. Hell, call Colt. That's if he and the little scientist can get reception wherever the hell they are right now," Emmett said, looking at Maverick with a wealth of understanding.

"Houston, Texas, last I checked. Avery's working with those scientists at NASA or something," Tanner filled in.

Clenching the brush in his hand, Mav said, "Look, just because we've slept together a few times, doesn't mean—"

All three of his friends laughed uproariously, like it was the funniest thing they had ever heard. Fuckers.

While those morons were carrying on, Lincoln sidled up to the stall and asked, "What the hell's so funny? Are we throwing a party and I wasn't invited?"

"It looks like Mav's gonna be the next one of us to take the plunge." Emmett guffawed and slapped Tanner on the back.

"Is that the case? With the gal from London?" Lincoln asked, his brows raised in question.

Tanner chuckled and nodded. "That's the one."

"Was there a meeting called that I wasn't aware of, gentlemen?" Amber stepped up by the stalls in one of her fancy business suits. Today, it was a deep, vibrant purple, and showed off her stellar legs. And while he didn't have any designs on his buddy Colt's baby sister, Mav wasn't dead, and could appreciate that she was a looker.

"Nah, we were just riding Mav," Tanner explained with a shake of his head.

"Oh, yeah? What about?" Amber asked, crossing her arms over her chest with the corners of her mouth curling up.

"On account of him and our British visitor getting real chummy. His truck has been parked outside her cabin a couple mornings this week," Emmett filled her in.

Maverick curled his hands into fists to keep them at his sides inside of boxing all their heads in. Some friends, to ride him this way—and in front of Amber. While Colt would have good-naturedly laughed it off, he wasn't in charge anymore.

"Is that so?" she asked, and shot him a glare. Normally she didn't mind him getting with a tourist here or there, but she had become friendly with Bianca.

"What it is, is none of y'alls damn business. I have a trail to lead. Unless you need me for something else?" Mav aimed the question in Amber's direction.

She shook her head. "No. I need Lincoln. If you would come with me, I have something I need you to look at."

Lincoln's expression turned frigid. He gestured. "Lead the way."

"Gentlemen. If you're done gossiping like a bunch of hens, we've got a ranch to run." Amber smiled. She left with Lincoln on her heels.

Maverick would never be able to figure how she could work in those dang things on the ranch.

"You know, I could always take her off your hands. She's quite the looker in those dandy jeans," Tanner teased.

Possessive fury rose in his chest. He slanted his gaze at Tanner and snarled, "Back the fuck off. Come anywhere near her, and you and I will have a problem."

Brows lifted in surprise at Mav's vehemence, Tanner lifted his hands. "Backing way the hell up. She's all yours."

"I've got work to do." Mav pushed out of Rosie's stall and strode off.

Emmett's final words trailed after him. "The dude is sunk, and he doesn't even realize it yet."

It was followed by Tanner's cackle. "Wait until Duncan returns from his overnight and hears this."

Idiots.

But then, the sinking sensation in the pit of his stomach had Mav worried. He didn't do relationships or exclusivity. And yet, here he was, thinking about her nonstop. Fantasizing about the number of ways he'd yet to take her and wanted to, feeling possessive and territorial.

His friends' words followed him onto the afternoon trail ride, and left him no clearer on his path forward.

19

*A*t the end of an incredibly long day, Maverick headed home in his truck. He bypassed Bianca's cabin as it came into view. He needed to prove to himself that he could stay away, and quit while they were ahead. Going cold turkey wouldn't be easy.

Especially given the mere sight of her cabin made him rock hard.

But he refused to let his dick do the thinking for him, he thought as he strode inside his cabin. Was it the most amazing sex of his life? Yes. Did he want to march himself out to his truck and drive to her place so he could have more of that off the charts sex? Also yes.

But would he allow himself to lose control? No. He was a Dom, for fuck's sake. He called the shots.

After a shower to wash off the dirt from the trail, and a spot of dinner, he relaxed on his leather couch in a wife beater and his boxers, watching a baseball game. It was one of his favorite sports to watch and play. He'd been an all-state pitcher his senior year of high school. He'd had scouts interested in him for farm teams.

Normally, a game would suck him in. Not tonight. His paltry excuses for not stopping at Bianca's place tonight weren't fooling him. Maybe he should have just gone to see her, he chided himself. She was only going to be in the country a few more weeks.

Would he regret not spending as much time with her as possible? Instead of worrying about his feelings and where it was going, shouldn't he be enjoying her? Soaking up every ounce of pleasure from their affair?

She was the elephant in the room, mocking him.

He startled at the knock on the front door. Who the hell could it be? Tanner had better not think he could swagger into Mav's place and drink his beer after the ribbing he'd given Mav today in front of Amber. Ready to tell whoever it was to get lost, he yanked the door open.

The breath whooshed from his lungs.

Bianca wore a black pea coat, her golden tresses spilled in loose curls over her shoulders. Her legs were bare from mid-thigh all the way down to a pair of sexy as hell red and black stilettos.

She was a fucking knockout. He was a damn idiot for not heading directly to her place.

Her fingers played with the belt of her coat. "Hi cowboy, going to let me in? Or are you just going to leave me out here on your stoop?"

"I wasn't expecting you. Come in." He pushed the door open wider to allow her inside. "I didn't realize you knew where I lived."

"I didn't, but I've become friends with the ranch owner, and she told me where I could find you." She shrugged and gave him a secretive smile as she entered, filling his cabin with her essence.

Closing the door on autopilot, his tongue stuck to the roof of his mouth as he studied her assessing his place before her eyes landed back on him. "I like your place. It suits you."

"For now, it does, until I've built my house. I'd like it to be larger, with a basement and a few more bedrooms, but I like the cabin style interior." Why the hell was he talking about the house he wanted to build and filling the air with small talk?

"Sounds nice."

He rubbed the back of his neck, unsure and fumbling, which was not like him at all. "Can I get you something to drink?"

"Maybe later," she replied, and that pink tongue of hers darted out to wet her lips.

"Then why are you—"

Holy fuck!

All his brain power drained from his head into his dick as she removed her coat. She was wearing only the heels and a seductive smile.

Entranced, he strode to her, every part of him attuned to her. "Do you always drive around in nothing but a coat and heels?"

He was pleased with himself for managing to string together a coherent sentence.

"Nope. I did this just for you, and for me. I wanted to see your reaction. It's one of my fantasies."

Lust riddled him. He was part of her fantasies. The knowledge that she was as mesmerized as he was obliterated any lingering concerns. His hands clasped her hips. "Yeah? One of mine is taking you in my bed. Put your arms around my neck, princess."

The moment she wound her arms around his neck, he

scooped her up, the game on the television forgotten. His reasons for not stopping at her place were in the trash.

To hell with it!

He fucking wanted her, more than he had ever wanted another woman. He couldn't explain it or quantify it. And he was done trying to keep himself from enjoying this splice of time with her.

He carried her into his bedroom and set her on the bed. "Stay there, I just need a few things."

Here at home, he had an entire BDSM arsenal in one chest of drawers. He grabbed the few items he wanted: nipple clamps, lube, butt plug, cuffs, and a flogger. He carted the haul over to the bed and said, "If anything I do hurts too much, use the safeword. Now that you're here, I want to try a few of the things I've fantasized about. And we'll get started on the one you told me about."

He held up the butt plug. He heard her breath catch.

She nodded and bent to remove the heels.

"Keep them on for now. They're sexy as fuck," he ordered as he slipped into Dom headspace.

He moved in and cupped her face in his hands. Those big blue eyes filled with longing as they stared at him. He lowered his mouth and brushed it gently over her lips. He didn't even use his tongue. He wanted to seduce her before he tied her up and flogged her.

Her hands splayed against his chest. Just that one little touch made his dick jerk.

And it was his signal to push her back and truly begin the scene. He lowered her onto her back, and wedged his hips between her supple thighs before he moved to her breasts. Curious how she would take the clamps, he sucked a pert nipple into his mouth as his hand plucked and twisted its twin.

Her fingers threaded into his hair as she arched her back, feeding him more of the mound. When the nipple protruded stiffly, he released it and picked up the Japanese clover clamps. The silver pair was connected by a thin chain. Keeping an eye on her reaction, he slipped the first one on.

Her eyes widened, pain slashed across her face. He bent forward and flicked his tongue over the abused nub.

She moaned, her gaze grew heavy, and she bit her bottom lip. Her response was all the encouragement he needed as he applied the same treatment to her other nipple. He loved her silky skin and sultry scent—it was some dark, mysterious scent that he had to get really close to smell. Her gasps of pleasure infused him, each one went directly to his dick and made it jerk. She was so passionate and responsive as she arched, trying to feed him the mound. She rocked her pelvis against his crotch. It took everything inside him not to rip away the barrier between them and plunge his staff in her hot, slick pussy. He could feel her wetness through his boxers. Knowing it was all for him, that he could make her this wild and needy, filled him with dark pride.

Fuck, he wanted to possess her in every way imaginable.

By the time he applied the second clamp, she was writhing and clawing at his back, her nails scoring his body from the force of her need. As much as he liked restraining a woman while he fucked her, he craved her mark on him, for it showed just how unrestrained and wild she became under his touch.

Needing skin to skin contact, he stood and ripped his shirt off. But he left his briefs on for the time being, to help him maintain control of the scene. What he wanted was to toss it all out the window and bury himself inside her.

"Get on your hands and knees for me, with that sweet ass of yours near the edge," he ordered, and helped her up.

Once he'd gotten her into position, he grabbed the bottle of lubricant, poured a healthy dollop in his hand, and parted her bottom to drip some onto her pretty pink rosette. She gasped as the liquid hit her naughty backchannel.

"Now, I want you to breathe for me. Take a few deep ones. I'm just going to stretch you a bit so you can take the plug tonight."

"Yes, Sir."

Encouraged by her compliance, he dipped his finger against the taut ring of muscles. To be the first to touch her virgin channel... He trembled as he circled the entrance, ensuring it was adequately lubricated.

"Breathe," he ordered, both for himself, as her ass muscles clamped down on his finger and he was barely able to penetrate her, and for her, because she was clenching at the intrusion.

When she obeyed, his finger slid in an inch. He bit back a groan. He couldn't wait to feel her ass around his cock, and prayed it would be something she enjoyed.

"Good. Again."

They worked together until he didn't have to instruct her to breathe any more. His index finger glided in and out without obstruction. Bianca gasped, and rocked back to meet his thrusting digit.

Oh, she liked it all right.

"Such a dirty girl, princess," he murmured, adding a second finger. Beginning the whole stretching process again.

He fought back the urge to shove his dick in her ass and fuck her. While he liked doling out pain, he didn't want it to be something that she would avoid or fear. When the dual fingers were thrusting in and out of her rear as she thrust her hips, trying to take more, he knew she was ready for the plug.

He removed his fingers from her bottom with regret, and wiped the lube off on the towel. He grabbed the smooth black tapered butt plug that was only a little larger than an inch in diameter at its base. He coated the device with lube before pressing the narrow tip at her back entrance. Her gasps of pleasure reached his ears as he slid it forward with little resistance. He thrust it in and out a few times, fucking her with it, watching the black silicone disappear into her tight hole. She was such a carnal woman, and matched his voracious, dark lusts.

Sliding it all the way in, he switched the vibrations on, and grinned darkly at her throaty moan.

"Give me your hands. I'm going to bind them behind your back, and then we're going to try the flogger."

She moved her arms quickly, like she wanted to please him. It puffed his chest with pride at how willing she was to submit and hand over her power. He affixed his cuffs around her wrists, thrilling at the way she looked with her hands bound at the small of her back, the butt plug deep in her ass, and dew coating the folds of her pussy.

She had her face resting on its side on the mattress. Her lips were parted, and her eyes were closed. Bliss covered her features.

He picked up the flogger with the soft leather falls. This was a gentler flogger that would introduce her to the sensation, and test whether she enjoyed the pain. Rubbing her bottom, he said, "I'm going to start with ten lashes of the flogger. If it gets to be too much, use your safeword. Understood?"

"Yes, Sir."

She shivered at his touch on her unblemished cheek—likely a combination of fear and excitement. Drawing the leather over her back like a caress, he smiled at her sigh. He lifted the tails and then, with a flick of his wrist, he brought the falls down across her butt. The slap against her flesh filled the bedroom. She jerked and her breath expelled in a rush. But she didn't use her safeword.

He applied a second and third swat, loving the way her milky skin turned pink. She gasped at each strike but didn't tell him to stop.

He kept an eye on her response to each lash, noting the way she tilted her hips up, and the slick dew coating her pussy. She was enjoying it, just like he knew she would. When he'd done ten, he rubbed the red marks he'd created and asked, "How are you, princess? Shall I keep going or would you like me to stop?"

"Don't stop, please, I need..." She whimpered, her voice thick with desire.

It was so fucking hot watching her surprise and pleasure at experiencing something that fell into the taboo category.

"I know what you need." He caressed her bottom for a moment before applying the flogger once again.

He struck her bottom with precision. When she tilted her hips up for more, he almost creamed in his boxers. Her moans grew in tenor as her bottom grew bright red. The moment he reached twenty lashes, he stopped. Just like with anything, it was better that he backed off on her first time experiencing it, and let her grow accustomed to it before taking it further.

Besides, he could no longer wait to take her. He felt his control slipping, and knew he couldn't go another moment without being inside her. He dropped the flogger onto the bed next to her, his body trembling with need.

Bianca pleaded, "Please."

"Hush, now. I'm going to slide my cock inside your tight pussy and make you feel so good," he crooned, and shoved his boxers down, letting them slide to the floor. The air was thick with lust as he positioned his body, spreading her legs a little more to give him ample room. Holding his aching shaft that was so hard he could drill nails with the damn thing, he rubbed the head through her soaked folds.

Her needy moans fueled his lust. He eased his dick inside, able to feel the plug in her ass, buzzing away. The plug made her cunt tighter so she clamped down on his cock. This could be an abbreviated performance on his part. Gliding deep, he furrowed his way in until his balls pressed against her clit.

Fuck.

The plug made her pussy so much tighter, he had to fight the waves of pleasure to keep himself from busting his nut immediately. Gripping her hips, he thrust, plunging in and out. This woman, with her fire and ice, captivated him, enthralled him—and, he very much feared, had altered him forever.

He could feel the shift inside him.

The sense of rightness and belonging, the click inside that told him she was it for him. That after her—if there was an after—no other woman would compare or measure up.

And those thoughts spurred him on as he fucked her. He knew he was rough as he pummeled her cunt. Her cries of pleasure drove him to increase his tempo. One of his hands snaked around her hip, and teased her clit while he pounded her cunt.

Mewls spilled from her mouth. Her pussy fluttered and clenched around him, signaling just how close she was to climaxing. Knowing he was nearing the edge of ecstasy himself, he leaned forward so that his chest lay flush against her back, with her bound hands between them. Sliding a hand around her throat, he pumped fast and furiously. Then he slid his hands down her chest, and gripped the clover clamps. Frantically plunging deep, he removed the clamps.

"Oh god!" She bucked at the pleasure-pain at their removal. The act catapulted her body over the ledge into bliss. She climaxed hard, clamping down on his dick. Electricity sizzled along his spine. His cock swelled. The orgasm detonated inside him.

"Oh fuck, princess," he roared and tossed his head back as he came, straining and pouring his essence inside her. The force of ecstasy obliterated him as it beat against his body. He quaked and trembled with his arms around her. Those little blissful sighs had him cupping her face and drawing it back. He slanted his mouth over hers while he was still buried deep inside her, needing the connection as he understood just how much she had altered his life in a few short days.

When he could finally breathe again, he lifted his mouth and regretfully withdrew his softening member. He turned the vibrations in the plug off before he removed it from her bottom and tossed it on the small towel. He undid the cuffs on her wrists, and rubbed her arms for a moment from her shoulders down so that she wouldn't be stiff from holding them in that position for so long.

"Stay there," he commanded. Taking everything into the bathroom, he laid it all on the counter then grabbed a washcloth and ran it under warm water.

He padded back into his bedroom, where she was still ass up in his bed where he'd left her. Using the cloth, he cleaned her crease, removing all the lube while he admired his marks on her bottom. Tossing the cloth in the hamper, he picked her up so that she was cradled against his chest, drew the covers down, and laid her down. Then he finally removed the sexy heels from her feet, and tossed them on the bench at the foot of the bed.

"I'll need those to get home," she murmured with a satiated smile curling her lips, her eyelids heavy.

"Tomorrow. You're staying tonight," he said, joining her in bed. There was no way he was letting her leave after this. And he didn't just mean his bed either, but his life.

Maverick drew her close, until her head rested against his chest and her slim leg was tossed over his. He'd never been much for cuddling after sex. Sure, he would provide aftercare once a scene was finished, but it had never been something that was more than part of the erotic act. But right now with Bianca, he needed the intimacy, realizing that she was the only one he wanted to experience this level of closeness with. "Come to the dance with me this weekend."

"What dance?" she asked, and shifted until those blue eyes looked up at him with her chin resting on his chest.

The warmth in those slate blue eyes had his arms tightening around her, afraid that she would somehow slip away.

"The one the ranch is hosting for guests. The employees all make an appearance," he explained.

"So, you're asking me on a date?" she asked her eyes full of affection.

Fear rattled him. He didn't date. It wasn't something he did. And even with the revelations that he was still trying to wrap his head around, he was uncomfortable admitting his deepening feelings. "It's not a date, it's a dance."

She cocked her head with a bemused expression.

"Okay, let me get this straight. You would like me to go with you to a dance."

"Yes." He nodded, not sure where she was going with this, but deciding he would play along.

"A dance that you're going to pick me up for?"

"Yes." Wasn't that what he had just said? Maybe her brain was still fuzzy from their lovemaking.

"A dance where you plan to introduce me to your friends, and dance with me?" she asked.

"Yes. That's what I said."

"Oh you silly, silly man. That's what we, in polite society, call a date." She laughed quietly.

Consternation filled him. Until he noticed the merriment in her eyes, and how she was biting back a smile.

"I'm going to make you pay for that, princess," he teased, with a pointed stare at her for being put in his place. So it was a date. That didn't mean he was altogether comfortable with it yet.

"I was counting on that." She snuggled against his chest as if she belonged there.

And he couldn't help but think: this was how it could be every night. Nor was he prepared for how much he wanted it—this—with her.

20

On Saturday evening, she stood before the beveled mirror in her bedroom, trying to calm the anxiety skittering along her spine.

She shouldn't be nervous.

Bianca had attended more than her fair share of dances over her lifetime. Stuffy, myopic gatherings that she had hated. She bet the dance tonight would be different to any she had attended before. As she checked her appearance in the mirror, she realized that it wasn't the dance so much as it was the man taking her that was causing the anxiety. After everything they had done, this outing was their first official date.

Much like for the land, she was falling for him. Falling so hard and so fast, it left her dizzy.

She had no business letting her heart get involved. On top of her engagement to Peter, the rugged cowboy was her total opposite in almost everything. He worked outdoors with his hands through rain or shine, and it made him tough and resilient. He had carved out a life to be proud of in spite of his difficult childhood.

But they had also discovered a few places where they were in alignment. Like their shared love of eighties metal, punk rock, and eighties movies. The last few nights, after they were spent and sated from lovemaking, they had watched a few of them. Last night, they'd viewed *Beast-master*, and had then role played a scene from the film in Maverick's bed.

Good lord, and the way he loved her! Madly, passionately, fulfilling every wicked fantasy she'd ever had. A simple, slanted glance from him, in what she was beginning to understand was his Dom mode, left her wanting to drag him into the bedroom or into a grove of nearby trees so he could have his way with her.

She put a hand over her jittery stomach, praying that the royal blue dress with the square neckline and blouson three quarter sleeves was the right one for tonight. What did one even wear to a dance on a ranch? She was about to find out. At least the neckline did wonders for her cleavage, sure to give Maverick teasing glimpses all night long. The fitted dress ended just above her knees. And she had added a pair of silver and black Louboutins with a four-inch heel that elongated her legs.

At the knock on the front door, she snapped her small clutch purse closed, turning the light off as she left the room, and headed to greet her date.

Her nerves reached a crescendo as she opened the door. All the breath whooshed from her lungs. The cowboy cleaned up really nicely. She slid her gaze over his crisp ivory dress shirt and black blazer down to the dark navy jeans, combined with his black Stetson and black boots.

Maverick's blank expression made her nerves heighten.

"Jesus Christ, princess!" He slapped a hand over his chest. "Give a guy a heart attack in that get up."

"You look good too. I almost don't recognize you without your plaid shirts."

He walked inside, his eyes never leaving her body. "I can clean up when I have to. But Jesus, you're fucking gorgeous. I'm almost tempted to say to hell with the dance."

Her breath caught at his compliment. "But won't it be better, building up the anticipation?"

A seductive, dark gleam filled his visage. "I bet I could convince you otherwise."

His low bedroom tone was like a sinuous caress down her spine. "While I'm sure you could, just imagine how grateful I will be by the time we leave the dance."

He cocked a dark brow. "How grateful we talking, princess?"

"I'd be your willing slave. On board with whatever dirty deeds you have in mind," she promised him. She would be up for that without the dance.

But she also wanted this night out with him, their date. It made their relationship real, having other people see them together. Even if they parted ways in a few weeks and she returned to England, she wanted this night with him to add to her memory banks that might have to see her through a lifetime.

Maverick's golden gaze smoldered. He grabbed her hand. "Let's go."

He made sure the front door was shut and locked, never releasing her hand. She balanced on her toes so that her heels didn't sink into the grass. He escorted her to the passenger side door and held it open. She struggled with the dress skirt for a minute as there wasn't a lot of stretch in the material.

"Um, I'm having some difficulties here. Give a girl a hand."

Maverick shook his head and feigned exasperation as he lifted her up and deposited her on the seat. "Anything else I can do for you, princess?"

"I'm good for now."

He closed the truck door. She watched his long-legged gait as he rounded the front and joined her in the truck's cab.

"How was your day at the stables?" she asked.

"Busy. I think Sunshine misses seeing you there," he said, and kept glancing her way, taking his gaze off the road.

"What is it? Why do you keep looking at me like that?"

He pulled into a vacant parking spot near the hotel and shifted the truck into park. Then he shot her a heated stare. "I just can't get over you in that dress."

"Why? Does it look bad? Is it the wrong type of dress for a dance here? Take me back home, and I can change." Anxiety battered her. It was from a lifetime of having her mother disapprove of her outfits.

"No. That's not what I mean at all. It's the fact that I'm going to be beating men away with a stick to keep you to myself tonight." He lifted her hand up and brushed his lips over the back.

"Oh, is that all?" Tension released from her body. He really liked the dress. He wasn't going to make her change.

"Let's get inside before I decide I want to find out what you're wearing beneath that thing," he murmured.

Maverick came around to the passenger door and helped her out of the truck. With his arms around her as he set her feet on the ground, she leaned up and whispered by his ear, "Not a stitch."

"Oh fuck." At his low male groan, she smiled. But then he nuzzled her neck and she was the one sighing, thinking maybe they should hurry back to her cabin.

Maverick straightened and cast her a sinful smirk. It let her know in all of two seconds that whatever he was planning for tonight would be fucking filthy and depraved, and that she would love every minute of it.

The lobby of the hotel had been decorated with flowers to fit in with the Spring Fling Dance in the ballroom. Country music spilled out of open doors. When he ushered her inside the ballroom, the dance was already in full swing. People were out on the dance floor doing the two-step. As she scanned the event, she realized just how overdressed she was as he steered her through to a table that was already full.

But she recognized some of the people there.

"Bianca, I'm so glad you could make it tonight," Amber said, rising, and came over to give her a hug. Bianca felt a smattering of relief that she wasn't the only one dressed up in something other than jeans. Amber wore a sleek, eye-popping red number and cheetah print stilettos that she envied.

"I wouldn't have missed it," she replied.

Grace stood in a silky, mint green sheath dress, right behind Amber, and took a turn hugging her. "The three of us really need to do a girls' night. I love your shoes."

"She brought enough of them with her," Maverick teased. "Amber, Grace, good to see you. Grace, I see you haven't decided to toss Emmett over and run away with me."

Emmett put an arm around Grace's waist. "She likes me too much. Just last night, she was saying—"

Grace put her hand over her husband's mouth. "Nothing they need to hear."

Emmett chuckled at his wife as she removed her fingers. "It's nice to see you again, Bianca."

"Likewise." She nodded at the hunky cowboy.

"Let me introduce you to the rest of the guys. You likely remember Tanner. Beside him is Noah, then Duncan, and on the end there is Lincoln," Maverick explained. Each man was rugged and fit.

So that was Lincoln. Bianca could see why Amber had the hots for him. He was almost as hot as her cowboy with his dark good looks. But she assessed all of Maverick's friends. The big, black-haired Duncan had an edge of danger rolling off him, while Noah's kind smile didn't reach the loneliness in his hazel eyes.

She gave them a friendly smile. "It's nice to meet you all. Good to see you again, Tanner."

She got a lot of nods and *ma'am*s.

"Would you like a drink?" Maverick asked loudly over the music.

"Sure. Just some white wine would be fine," she replied.

Maverick glanced at the group. "Anyone else need anything? Amber? Grace?"

"I'll take another white wine," Amber said, holding up her nearly empty glass.

"Nothing for me. Thanks," Grace said with a small shake of her head.

Amber asked Grace, "Why aren't you drinking? Last dance, Emmett had to carry you out."

Grace and Emmett shared an intimate look, one that Bianca was sure was the same look married couples had been giving each other for centuries. Emmett just grinned as Grace seemed a bit flustered and then turned to the group. "We were going to wait a bit longer to say anything, but I'm not drinking tonight, nor will I be for about the next seven months or so."

Amber gasped. "You're pregnant?"

Grace nodded. "We are."

Emmett pressed his lips against her temple as congratulations erupted around the table. There was a lot of back slapping from the cowboys for Emmett, and gentle hugs for Grace, like they were all worried they would break her in her delicate state.

The joy of it got to Bianca. It was infectious, and such a far cry from how the news would be received in her inner circles back home, where there would be whispers and tight smiles, insincere felicitations.

This, right here, was what she wanted for her life. The friendships and camaraderie that were genuine and meaningful. It was how life should be. And those seeds Maverick had planted within her, about staying here instead of heading back to London, began to grow.

While Maverick was getting their drinks, Tanner sidled up beside her. "Want to dance?"

The music changed into an up-tempo number.

"But I don't know the steps." She watched the boot stomping crowd.

"Not to worry, I can show you." Tanner held out a hand and cast her a lopsided, friendly grin. His enthusiasm was infectious.

"What the hell." She placed her hand in his. Tanner led her out and proceeded to twirl her around the dance floor until she was laughing up at him. Her feet didn't hit all the right steps, but no one cared. It was freeing, and she lost herself in the joviality.

No one here was judging her that she wasn't up to snuff with the dances.

As the evening progressed, Bianca danced not just with

Tanner, but Lincoln, Noah, and Duncan. Even Trevor, whom she remembered from the stables, asked her for a dance. She even did a two-step with Emmett before Maverick swooped in and claimed her for another slow dance.

He held her close, his hands on her lower back.

"You look like you're having fun," he murmured as they swayed around the dance floor.

"I am. Thank you for bringing me. I like your friends." Which was odd, because she rarely liked a guy's friends. Some of Peter's friends were downright idiotic blokes.

"They're not bad. It's winding down for the night. We can stay until the end if you would like."

She leaned up on her toes and murmured into his ear, "I'd like you to take me home and proceed with whatever wicked fantasy you had in mind for tonight... Sir." She purred the last bit.

His hands tightened against her. "And if I had another place in mind that I wanted to take you, would you be up for that?"

Her heart stuttered. "Yes."

God! She was game for anything the man could drum up.

"Then let's go, because I can't wait any longer to have my hands all over you," he admitted. His gaze smoldered with promised ecstasy, and tripped her body into overdrive. Flutters erupted deep in her belly.

They hadn't even started, and she was already on fire. "How fast can we get there?"

A dark, seductive smirk spread over his lips. "You're about to find out, princess."

After saying goodbye to his friends who were still

present, since Grace and Emmett had already departed, Maverick quickly escorted Bianca out to his truck. Anticipation hummed in her veins. She couldn't wait to see what he had planned.

21

*M*averick pulled up and parked the truck just outside Cabin X. After he'd asked Bianca to the dance, he had reserved it for the two of them tonight. The secluded lodge was off limits to outsiders. Only someone with an access code could enter. And when one of the members wanted the cabin for the night, they booked it.

Emmett had brought Grace here. Colt had brought Avery here when they had been at the ranch over the Christmas holidays.

And now Mav was bringing Bianca. Perhaps it was a rite of passage.

"Where are we?"

"This is Cabin X, a private cabin my friends and I keep for some of our extracurricular activities." He laid the innuendo on thick.

"So it's a BDSM haven?" she asked with obvious interest.

"Pretty much. Ever seen one?" he asked, because he was always surprised by some of her responses.

"No. But I have friends in London who attend house sex parties." She shrugged like it was no big deal.

"Really? Did you ever go with those friends?" He was curious because of how adventurous she was with him.

A shadow passed over her face. "No. If it would have ever leaked out that I attended one, I never would have heard the end of it from my mother."

Bianca was a grown woman. Yet the mention of her mother seemed to make her light dim and cause some of her independent spirit to fade. The woman couldn't be that bad, could she? "And she has that much sway over what you do?"

"No. Not anymore. I won't let her."

Her firm resolve made him want to cuddle her. She was trying to toss off the shackles of her old life. He knew just how much work that took, and was so damn proud of her. It was why he wanted to bring her here tonight. This was his way of claiming her, and as much of a declaration of his intentions as he was ready to admit. "Now when we go inside, we're going to do a scene. If at any time you want things to stop, I expect you to use your safeword. Got it?"

"Yeah... Maverick?" she said before he climbed out of the truck.

He shot her a glance. "Yeah?" he asked, worried that she might back out of the evening he had planned.

"I'm glad you asked me to go to the dance with you. Thank you for that. It was the best night."

He leaned across the console, cupped her nape, and planted his mouth over hers, letting his need and hunger for her fill his kiss. She moaned into his mouth and gripped the lapels of his sport coat.

Need clawed against his resolve. What she did to him, the way she tied him up in knots, and left him aching to be inside her with a mere kiss, was everything he hadn't realized had been missing in his life. She filled holes inside him that he hadn't been aware were even there.

He tore his mouth from hers, breathing heavily, ready to rip her dress off and have her ride him. But he pulled the frantic, greedy edges back, lassoing them under control.

"Let's get you inside before I decide to fuck you in my truck."

"I honestly wouldn't mind," she admitted with a half laugh.

Jesus. The thought of pulling her onto his lap and letting her ride him, had his dick straining painfully against his jeans.

"I'll keep that in mind for the future. But I want you inside, and naked." He vaulted out of his truck and quickly strode to the passenger side, on edge, and eager for the night ahead.

———

MAVERICK USHERED Bianca inside what he'd dubbed Cabin X. The exterior looked like all the other cabins on the property.

But that was where all similarity ended. The moment they stepped inside, she shivered at the erotic cornucopia. Instead of couches and end tables and flatscreen TVs, the cabin was littered with high end BDSM furniture.

She felt Maverick's gaze on her as she walked through the place, studying each piece. Some were crystal clear as to what their function was and how they were to be used. Others, not so much.

"Go ahead and look around while I get the station we're going to use prepared. You've got five minutes before I want you at the upright stockade," Maverick said, his voice laced with lust, and nodded at the wood contraption.

She nodded. "Yes, Sir."

Her curiosity driving her, she just wanted to peek inside the rooms. There were three bedrooms, and she wondered what type of furniture was housed in each. She poked her head inside them. There was a weird-shaped cross in one, a padded table and bench in another. And in the last one... she had no idea what it was other than it looked like a wood and leather version of a weights bench with a few modifications. At the end of the short hall, there was a bathroom, and an entrance to a stairwell that led down to a basement.

"That leads to the dungeon. We're not going to use it tonight," Maverick said behind her.

While she was curious, she was more than ready to get started with whatever he had cooked up. She turned his way and smiled. While she had been exploring, he had removed his hat, blazer, and shirt.

Her gaze caressed the muscled expanse of his chest. Her fingers itched to touch him and she sauntered his way, enjoying the thrill of watching his eyes go dark with lust as she approached.

"Ready?" He quirked a brow.

"Lead the way, Sir."

He ushered her over to the glossy mahogany stockade with padded black leather covering various points.

"I want you to take off the dress but leave the heels on. They're sexy as fuck."

She gave him her back and asked, "Would you help me with the zipper?"

Hands lightly touched her elbows. He caressed up her biceps and over her bare shoulders, down to the tiny zipper in between her shoulder blades. He lowered it slowly. And she hid her smile when he issued a passionate, "Fuck, you weren't lying. You went to the dance full commando."

She glanced at him over her shoulder. "Had to with this dress to avoid panty lines."

She let the material slide down her body and pool at her feet. A hand shot out in front of her and he was lifting her up, taking her the remaining few feet. The carnal light in his gaze made her shiver.

He helped her get situated with her feet on a raised platform, where he buckled cuffs around her ankles to keep her feet in place. There was a padded leather cushion that was adjusted so that her belly rested against it as she was bent at a forty-five-degree angle. Her wrists were imprisoned in cuffs attached to the top bar of the stockade, and then she had a collar snapped in place around her neck. To round out the restraints, and keep her from moving at all, a leather strap was affixed around her waist.

She watched Maverick double check all the cuffs, ensuring that they weren't too tight.

He'd barely touched her. All he had done was restrain her body. And she was going up in flames. She was wet. She could feel the slick moisture building as her pussy throbbed.

Then he was behind her, spread her labia wide, and pressed the head of a wand vibrator against her pussy.

Oh fuck!

Maverick switched it onto a low vibration setting—just enough to turn her on and keep her on edge, but not fast enough to make her climax. And then he was pouring lube on her back entrance, smearing it around the puckered ring.

"Relax, princess. Deep breaths for me. I'm just going to insert a plug to help stretch you a bit while our scene takes place—that way, when I've finished paddling your ass, I can fuck it."

She groaned. Who knew that she would enjoy anal play? Ever since the first time with the plug, he had been increasing the size and shape each night, explaining that when he did slide his cock inside, he wanted her experience to be pleasurable.

She exhaled as his fingers pressed forward into her forbidden channel. The combination of the vibes against her pussy and his fingers gliding deeper and deeper in her ass were simply exquisite.

She moaned when he replaced his thrusting fingers with the bulbous head of the plug. It was thicker and wider than any he had used on her thus far. It stretched her back channel near the point of pain and discomfort.

Maverick thrust the device deeper and deeper, fucking her ass with it, likely imagining what his cock would look like plunging deep into her rear.

She groaned as the plug slid all the way in.

"Fucking beautiful, princess. You're doing so well." His work-roughened hands caressed her back from her shoulders to her bottom, and squeezed. "Remember to use your safeword if you need it. I'm using a simple silicone paddle to get you accustomed to how it feels. That way we can see if it's something that you like, since you enjoyed the flogger so much."

God, did she ever. That had been one of the hottest nights of her life. But then, they all were with Maverick.

He stopped caressing her bottom with his hands. Against her rear, the cool press of the silicone rubbed in circles over her cheeks. She almost laughed, wondering how this was supposed to be painful when it sort of tickled and turned her on. However, she had a feeling if she did, she would pay for it. His movements were hypnotic.

The first slap against the butt was almost playful, teasing, and made her wonder what the fuss was all about. But she should have known there was more coming. With her cowboy, there always was more.

It was his way of easing her in, lulling her, and studying her reactions, before he increased the pace and force behind the whacks. With each successive crack of the paddle across her bottom, her eyes would widen at the slice of pain. It hurt, but it was a good hurt.

"How you doing, princess?" Maverick asked, running a palm over her burning flesh.

"Good, Sir."

"Okay, then, I'm going to go a bit harder and see how you do."

"Yes, Sir."

The next whack made her eyes water. Pain radiated up and down her spine. It was like a pebble being tossed into a still lake. The waves of it connected with the vibrations against her clit and the plug stretching her ass. It magnified the heat filling her to a thousand degrees.

On the next hard blow, the air expelled from her lungs and she moaned. "Oh my god!"

The pain was intense as it razored through her body, only to shift into pleasure more powerful than she had ever experienced. It was like she had to go through the pain to get the pleasure.

It hurt. She wasn't going to lie. The force of the next blow made the word explode from her mouth. "Shit!"

Lacerating waves pummeled her being. But she breathed through it, and found herself in this blissful, somewhat dreamy phase of heightened awareness and need lighting up her form.

But then the vibrations against her pussy stopped.

Maverick leaned over her back, massaging the burning globes of her rear. "You did so well. And as your reward, I'm going to fuck both your holes. Come as much as you need to, princess."

She moaned as she felt the head of his cock press against her pussy. He thrust, and was filling her. She was tighter because of the plug but loved the sensations. It was one of the reasons why he kept using them each night. It made the fit so much tighter, and let her feel his big dick even more.

Maverick pumped his cock, fucking her without reservation. Plunging deep inside, he gripped her hips as he pounded her cunt. One of his palms snaked around her hip and he rubbed his fingers over her swollen clit. With the combination of all the stimulation, in no time, Bianca's climax roared through her. The tidal wave slammed her form and left her quaking with ecstasy.

Before she had a chance to come down, Maverick withdrew his shaft. She whimpered at the loss. She loved the way he felt inside her. Then the plug was sliding out from her rear as he removed it. She had been overly full, and now was empty.

Although it would not be for long, she realized as fingers coated with lube slathered over her back channel. She trembled at the thought that this was finally it, the moment he would fuck her there. At the press of his cock against her rear entrance, she groaned as he slid the smooth crown an inch inside.

"Deep breaths for me. Relax, and let me in." He murmured the silky command.

One hand played with her pussy, stroking her sensitive nub while he thrust and retreated, furrowing deeper and deeper with each pass. She clenched her hands into fists at the amazing sensations flooding her system. Every nerve ending was electrified.

It felt tight, rode the line of pain, and different than when he was inside her pussy. But it was no less pleasurable. In fact, it was incredible and depraved. And it seemed like there was this depth of ecstasy that was just out of her grasp.

On the next thrust, he penetrated her fully, completely embedded in her ass. She could feel his cock throbbing.

"Jesus, you feel like hot fucking silk clamping my dick," he growled, pulled back slowly until just the tip remained, and then thrust all the way in until his balls pressed against her clit.

Intense, delicious pleasure flowed and pulsed through her. She moaned. "More."

She needed him to move faster, get her body closer to that glimmering precipice of ecstasy just out of her reach.

He leaned forward, cupped and kneaded her tits. And then he began to fuck her ass, slow and steady. Pleasure blasted her body. She trembled and quaked, unable to do more than take the heady fucking. Mewls spilled from her mouth unimpeded. But he continued his slow and steady assault.

"Sir, faster, please," she begged, desperate and needing release.

He sped his thrusts up a teensy bit. "Like this, princess?"

She couldn't even shake her head. It was better, but still wasn't enough. "No, more."

Maverick gripped her breasts painfully, enough so that there would be bruising on them. She loved that he was marking her skin, leaving behind reminders of their mating.

His tempo increased, driving her desire up higher, spiraling through her body. "How's this?"

It wasn't nearly enough to send her overboard. She needed that release. Through gritted teeth, she stated, "I need you to fuck me, hard and fast, Sir."

Her naughty words were the match that ignited a forest fire. They decimated his control, and the tether holding him back snapped. And Maverick did exactly as she had asked. He fucked her. Pounded his cock in hard, brutal digs. His hips slammed against her bruised, burning backside.

"Oh." Ragged moans spilled from her mouth.

Maverick was raw and savage as he screwed her. He grunted as his staff hammered her channel. The rigorous slap of flesh and deep thrusts left her gasping at the intensity. She clenched her hands at the building rapture. Her pussy fluttered and clenched as pleasure poured from her ass to her sex.

Without warning, Maverick smacked the hood of her clit. Euphoric-filled bursts set off a chain reaction. And she came, harder than she had ever come before.

"Oh god," she keened as her body dissolved under the tectonic force of ecstasy battering her body.

"Fuck, princess." Maverick slammed home, his cock juddered and spilled his seed, filling her ass as he thrust through his climax.

But the pleasure of the scene and world-altering sex had taken a toll. Her eyelids closed. Her limbs were heavy as she floated sublime in bliss. In her haze, she felt him withdraw his shaft from her well-used body.

Distantly, Maverick moved around behind her. A cool cloth wiped through her crease, startling her, removing the lube and his spunk. But then she sighed as he took care of her, like he did every night. Next, her restraints were removed, starting with her ankles, then her waist, and then her neck. His hands were so gentle as they moved over her flesh, it made her feel cherished.

When he freed her wrists, she stood, glad that she was no longer bent over. But the night had caught up with her and she was sliding down, her legs too weak to hold her up. Strong arms caught her before she crashed into a limp pile on the floor.

"I've got you, princess. Just close your eyes and let me care for you." He pressed his lips against her forehead, much in the same way Emmett had done with Grace.

And that little kernel flooded her with hope. Perhaps she really did have a future outside what her mother dictated. A life that she built, one that might even include Maverick.

Content, blissful, happier than she ever remembered being, she rested her head against his firm shoulder, sighed, and cuddled into in his warmth.

---

22

*O*ver the course of the next week, Bianca spent her days painting, and her nights with Maverick. There were even a few days when he stopped by for a quick lunch, which meant a hard and fast tumble in her bed, or on the sofa, or even up against the front door.

On the days Maverick didn't stop by, she met him at the stables for a trail ride, and they would inevitably wind up at his property. There was a particular thicket of trees that was a favorite for them, it kept them shrouded from observers as they made love.

He was the most amazing lover, dominant to be sure, but he also made her heart tremble and wish for things. She was in love with him. And not just a little bit, but great big, scary, deep in her bones, in love with Maverick.

Falling for him hadn't been part of the plan, but there was no way around it. In short order, he had changed her entire world.

And she had a plan.

Before she divulged everything—including the engagement with Peter—she had to see if he had feelings for her too. While he had mentioned wanting to keep her, it had been said in the heat of the moment. She needed to discover what he would think if she stayed in Colorado. Thoughts of London, her mother, and the wedding, of leaving it all behind, filled her with unrivaled joy. Ending the engagement would be difficult because she did consider Peter a friend, but it was the right thing to do. She couldn't marry him when she was headlong in love with another man.

Bianca understood what a cock up it was, and that it wouldn't go over well. But she couldn't go through with it. There was nothing for her in England and everything for her here. It was the place where she had found herself again.

And more importantly, she had found her heart. The part of herself she had started to believe no longer existed.

Until Maverick.

Which was why she had picked up dinner from the steak place in town. As much as she might wish she could be Betty Homemaker, if she tried cooking a meal like the one she was going to serve him, she'd likely set the cabin on fire. By accident, of course, but when it came to cooking, she was a lost cause.

For now.

Because if she was going to live here, she would need to become more self-sufficient. That included doing things like cooking. From what she had learned on the Internet and after asking Amber what winters were like here, she knew she wouldn't be able to run into town in the dead of winter when she needed sustenance for the two of them.

She pressed a hand over her rapidly beating heart as she set the table. And then she heated up the meal in the oven, just like the chef had instructed. She tossed the salad and put it on the table with the bread as dinner warmed, then got out the bottle of Macallan, figuring this was a night of seduction with the man she loved, and she wanted to make it memorable.

At the knock on the door, she shivered. "It's open."

She pulled the meal out of the oven, pleased by the look and scent. Maverick strode inside, removing his hat, and froze after he shut the door.

"Something wrong?" she asked, carting the dish with the steaks over to the trivet on the table.

"You look edible. And you cooked?" he asked, his gaze skimming the meal and then returning to her.

"I can't take credit for the food. I only heated it up. It's from that steak place in town."

"Are we celebrating something?"

Her heart sped up. She wanted to seduce him first before she told him. "Do I have to have a reason to want to have a nice dinner with you with the hope that you'll ravish me afterward?"

He finished removing his boots, depositing them by the door, just beneath the hook where he'd hung his hat. A grin tugged at his lips as he eradicated the distance and slid his hands over her hips to pull her close. "No, it's nice. Unexpected and appreciated, because I'm starving. Didn't have a chance to stop for lunch today. And like you have to ask about the ravishing."

His hands caressed her back in gentle circles as he lowered his mouth over hers, making a point that he needed no enticing to ravish her. She poured herself into the kiss.

She stopped him before it grew too much, and they lost their heads. Breathing heavily, she said, "I'm glad you like it. I missed lunch as well."

"Well, can't have you wasting away now, can we? Let me just go wash my hands, and I'll join you." He kissed her again, quickly this time, and released her with a playful swat to her bottom.

He strode down the hall to the bathroom. It gave her time to finish getting their meal on the table and the scotch into glasses. When he joined her back at the table, she couldn't help but think that this was how it could be.

Oh, she knew some of the enjoyment would wear off. Reality and day-to-day living would ensue after the honeymoon period on their affair passed. But she wanted that with him—the day-to-day stuff.

"So, did you finish that piece from the other day?" he asked as he held out the chair for her to take her seat. Then he joined her at the table.

She served the salad, putting generous helpings in each bowl. "I did. In fact, when I went into town this afternoon, I took one of my pieces to Archie's as a gift."

"Oh yeah? That was nice of you. Did he like it?" Maverick asked as he took a sip of the whiskey and pleasure filled his face.

"You could say that. His wife apparently runs the art gallery in town. And they want to display some of my work."

A smile split his face. "That's amazing, princess. Congrats, it's well deserved. Your work is beautiful. And see, the dinner is for a celebration."

"Yeah, I guess you're right. I wasn't thinking about that when I was arranging the dinner though. His wife is going to come one day next week to look at what I have, to see which ones they would like to show."

He took her hand in his and lifted it up to his mouth, brushing a kiss over the back. God, he made her sigh with little gestures like that. "I'm proud of you."

Oh, he was going to make her cry. She blinked back the sudden sheen of tears.

"What? Did I say something wrong?"

She shook her head, incredibly moved by him. "No. It's just, no one has ever said that to me before."

His eyes softened. "Ah, I see. Well, it's true, and I am proud of you. Now, how will it work, since you will be heading home in two weeks?"

She took a drink of the scotch to steady herself. "That's something I wanted to ask you. How would you feel if I extended my stay? I've already asked Amber if this cabin is available for me to continue renting. I can rent it through the end of May. After that, she will have to move me to another unit."

"You could always stay with me, if you're planning on staying. I could clear out my spare room so you could keep painting." And the look in his eyes as he offered her the space... god, every woman should have a man look at her that way once in their lives.

Her heart soared. Overjoyed, she smiled and asked, "Really? You wouldn't mind me staying in your man-cave and disrupting your life that way?"

"Nope, it's been disrupted from the moment you sashayed into my life. And I can prove it to you." He tossed his napkin on the table and rose.

"But the meal—" she protested, gesturing at the spread on the table.

"Will still be there after I'm done with you." He drew her into his arms and hoisted her up. His mouth claimed hers for a deep, soul-stirring kiss that left her breathless. With his help, she wrapped her legs around his waist and felt the firm ridge of his desire for her. She moaned into his mouth as he carried her from the dining room into the bedroom.

Inside, he set her on her feet and tore his mouth off hers. Their hands rushed over one another, working to rid themselves of clothing, tugging at material and zippers until they were in nothing but their underwear as he pushed her onto the bed.

What began as a hot as hell mating shifted as Maverick settled between her thighs and slanted his mouth over hers. He savored her. His mouth moved softly, his caresses were tender, and he drew her into a sensual web full of sighs and wonder.

This wasn't only sex tonight. Oh, the extraordinary passion was still present, boiling and bubbling beneath the surface. But as his mouth and hands loved her, she knew what it was to be cherished. Her hands flowed over his back, marveling at the way his muscles rippled and flexed.

She sighed as he kissed his way down her body near her sex, then started over with her legs, beginning at her feet, moving first up one leg to the inside of her thigh, then treating the other with the same maneuvers.

He drew her panties off slowly. Fit himself between her thighs. Parted her folds and lapped at her sensitive flesh. He was gentle as he drove her body up. She clutched his head and shoulders as her pleasure grew. He bit down and she splintered, fracturing into a million bursts of pleasure.

Her back arched as she came, riding out the waves of ecstasy.

And when he finally slipped inside her, he cupped her face in his hands and took her mouth. She clung and moved with him, infusing her every touch, each caress, and kiss with her feelings. It was ironic how much he had come to mean to her, given their auspicious beginning. But she wouldn't have it any other way, she wouldn't have *him* any other way. Because to her, he was perfect, and everything she never realized she needed.

His hands found hers as the heat rose and their tempo increased. He threaded their fingers together. And deep in her heart, she knew he was it for her. She might have had to leave everything she knew behind, and travel half a world away to find him. But it had been worth it.

Their bodies crested in unison. Maverick tore his mouth from hers and stared deeply into her eyes. For a moment, it looked like he was going to say something. But he held back, choosing instead to kiss her once more, sweetly, to the point where she thought her heart was going to burst free from her chest, she was so happy.

Rolling them until he was on his back and she was cuddled along his side, he said, "This week, I can work on getting the furniture in the guest room moved. That way, we can move you in sooner."

"That would be amazing." She cupped his stubbled cheek.

He kissed her palm and said, "I'm glad you think so. Now I don't know about you, but I'm still hungry."

"Yeah, I could eat some more. There's dessert too," she offered, thinking of the chocolate mousse in the fridge.

"You mean, you weren't it?" he playfully teased.

"Maybe one of them. Come on. I'll show you. It's this chocolate mousse cake that's supposed to be excellent." She worked to untangle her limbs from his, and rise.

The moment her feet touched the floor, he said, "Only if I get to eat you afterwards as the encore."

"If you ask nicely," she replied as he stood at her side.

"Oh, I'm always nice, princess. Here, I'll show you." He

tackled her back into bed and had her squealing, and then moaning.

It was safe to say, it took them a bit longer to move from bed back out into the kitchen, where they heated everything up in the microwave and ate naked. Once the dishes were clear and in the dishwasher, Maverick carried her back to bed, where they tumbled exhausted into sleep.

But throughout the long night, they turned to one another again and again. The newfound closeness, the prospect of extending their time together, and yes, even her staying in his place, which was a huge step forward, brought about a need to continue the night. Almost like they were afraid it would all disappear come morning.

Until they finally slept the deep sleep of the sated, with their limbs entwined.

23

"*A*re you sure I can't convince you to go another round, princess?" Maverick stood with the hot shower spray beating down on his shoulders, looking like sin.

"As tempting as that is, I need a little break, or I won't be able to walk today."

He flashed a sexy, inherently male grin her way. "I bet I could change your mind."

The man could convince the Holy Mother to commit atrocities with that smile. Bianca's heart fluttered in her chest. "While I'm certain that you could do that, I still want to go for that trail ride today. I've missed Sunshine."

He sighed. "I guess we can go for a ride. It will just give me time to work on my fantasy for tonight."

Her belly fluttered and clenched in delicious ripples. "I'm sure whatever you dream up, I will like."

There was a knock at the front door that interrupted them.

"I'll get it," Bianca said.

"It's probably Tanner. He had something he wanted to

bring by, and I told him I would be here. I'll be out in just a minute. I need to take care of something first." He glanced down at his erection.

The insistent knocking made her roll her eyes, when what she really wanted to do was go back into the shower with him for round two, and to help him with his problem.

She donned her robe figuring that with Tanner, she could let him in really quickly and excuse herself to go and change. And she thought it was amazing that Mav was being this open with their relationship—that he was telling his friends where he could be found.

Bianca had a big grin on her face, feeling like her life was finally everything she wanted it to be as she opened the door. The smile froze as she stared at the person standing on her doorstep. "Mother."

Gwyneth Peabody looked as out of place in her Gucci loafers, pressed trousers, and Prada bag as a black bear in a tea room. She strode right on in without invitation, leaving Bianca to close the door behind her. Her mother's frosty glare assessed the cabin before it landed on her, her frown deepening when she took in the state of Bianca's hastily donned robe. "Finally. I had to travel five thousand miles to put an end to your nonsense. Pack your things, you've been gone long enough. It's time to return to London."

Thinking of who was in her shower, Bianca's internal panic button blared. "I'm not ready to go anywhere. I like it here, and plan on staying."

She hated that her mum was here, tainting a place Bianca had come to love with her presence.

Her mother rolled her eyes. "Really Bianca, I have had it with this rebellion of yours. It is well past time you pull your act together and start acting like a Peabody."

The padded footsteps against the hardwood had Bianca

digging her nails into her palms. This was going to pot so quickly, it was like a disaster film. She could see the wreck coming but had no way to stop it. Maverick strolled out of the bedroom in his jeans, his shirt unbuttoned and loose over his big frame, and barefoot, with his hair still wet.

Her mother's gaze zeroed in on Maverick as he came to stand beside Bianca, like he was giving her a show of support. Her mum lifted a brow, her eyes filled with derision. "I see why you've not been answering my calls. It's all very well and good that you've got this out of your system. But playtime with the help is over."

Bianca sucked in a breath, her fury rising. "Mother, don't speak to him like that. You have no right."

"I will speak to him however I want to, my dear, especially when the man has clearly been intimate with my engaged daughter."

In a single phrase, her mother had exposed Bianca's secret, the one she had been planning on telling him and explaining. Her heart plummeted into her toes. Maverick's face hardened to stone, his narrowed gaze sliced her way. "Engaged?"

She swallowed the lump in her throat as she watched him erect walls between them. She didn't want to explain this with her mother observing the scene. Her mum always ruined everything for her. Panic engulfed her as she fought to find the right words.

Her mother smiled with a gleam Bianca knew all too well. "Well, of course, she's been engaged to Peter since she was thirteen. They've both had their fun, but now it's time they got serious about their future. It's not every day one's daughter marries the son of a duke, and a member of the House of Lords."

"Well, then. I will be out of your hair. So you can get

back to your fiancé. Have a pleasant flight back to London." The furious glare in Maverick's eyes left her heart aching as he stormed past her. He grabbed his boots and hat, then stalked out before she could say anything, before she could explain, slamming the door on his way out.

The moment he was gone, Bianca rounded on her mother and spat, "How could you?"

"You've already embarrassed this family for long enough. I will do what I must to protect our interests and our standing. People are already beginning to talk about your disappearance."

Like Bianca gave a flying fuck what any of those people thought any longer.

"And if I don't want to go with you?" In this moment, she hated her mother. What kind of mother hurt their child on purpose? It was all she had ever done to her.

"What do you have here? Some backwoods country bumpkin? Honestly, Bianca, do you really think he could make you happy?" her mother chided.

Yes. Yes, she did. With everything inside her, Bianca knew that man could make her deliriously happy for the rest of her life. It didn't matter that they were complete opposites. With what they both brought to the table, it balanced them out, and made her feel whole for the first time in her life.

At least, she had believed that until her mother ruined it with her well laid, barbed words. She snapped, "Like you know anything about what I want or need."

Her mum's eyes, so like her own, narrowed. "Here's what I do know. You're going to pack your things and come with me now, or you will be cut off."

"I don't need your money. I have my own." She had quite a bit of it, in fact. Money that she had inherited and invested well. She was set for the rest of her life, and only had to work if she chose to do so.

"You do. But when I say you will be cut off, I mean you will be written out of our wills. All our holdings, like the estate, will go to charities, and distant relatives will inherit our title. And you will get nothing."

Bianca didn't care about their money, but the family home... It had been a part of their family for ten generations. She had one day hoped her children would get to visit, and perhaps call it home. "But you're making me marry a man I don't love."

Victory lit her mother's eyes. "Tosh, what does love have to do with anything? You have a duty to your family to uphold the name, and not cause us any further disgrace."

Bianca could feel it—the parts of herself that had been free here in the wilds of Colorado began to retreat inside her. All the hope and excitement she had felt not thirty minutes ago for her future dimmed as the cage bars closed around her once more.

She was bound for a life of tedium and loneliness.

Not that it really mattered; she would be leaving her heart here. "I'll go with you, on one condition. I need to go and talk to Maverick first. He deserves an explanation from me without you around."

"Pack your things and get dressed, then I will have the driver take you to wherever he is, and you can say your goodbyes. Take it or leave it."

"Fine." Bianca headed back to her room and slammed the door shut, flipping the lock so she could dress and manage a brief moment of privacy.

She called Amber while she did so.

"Hey, I'm glad you called. Grace and I were thinking about a tame girls' night next weekend, since the mommy to be can't drink. We figured an eighties romcom retrospective, *Pretty in Pink*, that type of thing," Amber said.

It sounded wonderful. And Bianca had to fight back her tears that she wasn't going to get a chance to say goodbye in person. "I wish I could. My mother's here, and I have to return to London today. I want you to charge me for the full five weeks, plus the deposit. And any extra needed to dispose of things that are left behind. I may not be able to take everything with me."

"What's going on? Did you and Maverick have a fight?" Amber asked, her voice filled with concern.

Bianca blinked back the tears. She couldn't fall apart. "I'm sure he'll tell you anyway. I have to go back because I'm engaged. I don't love Peter, but it doesn't seem to matter. I'm sorry I lied to everyone. You guys are wonderful."

"Well, have a good flight. I've got things I need to do," Amber said coldly.

A tear slipped out as Bianca said, "I'm so sorry I lied. Amber, you and Grace were the first friends I've ever had who liked me for me."

Amber sighed. "Look, I'm not going to pretend I understand your reasons for lying. But you can call me when you get back to London because that's what friends do. Then you can explain to me why you lied. Besides, I've never been, and might be up for a visit if I ever get a vacation around here."

"Bye, Amber. Thanks, for everything." She hung up, and swiped at her tears.

And then she proceeded to pack in record time. She snuck in the plaid shirt Maverick had left behind last week. It smelled like him still, and almost brought her to her knees.

When her luggage was packed, she headed into her art room, and her heart bled at the sight of everything inside it.

"What's taking so long, Bianca?" Her mother strode into the room and cast a spurious glance at her art. "Leave it. You won't have any need for any of it in London. Once the wedding and honeymoon are over, then it will be time for the real work to begin. You'll be so busy, there will be no time for any of these frivolous pursuits. I've already called the rental car company. They have someone coming to pick the car up today. I had the driver take the keys to the hotel reception desk for them to pick up."

Defeated and heartbroken, Bianca followed her mum outside the cabin, leaving the cabin's keys on the kitchen table.

She stared at the small building where she had lived these past few weeks and rediscovered herself before she slid into the back seat of the limo while the driver loaded the car with all her luggage. Her head swam as she tried to figure out what to say to Maverick when everything had gone sideways so fast.

At least her mother kept her promise and had the limo driver stop at the stables. Bianca knew that was where he would be, and spied his truck parked outside.

"Don't be too long, dear," her mum stated as she climbed out.

"It will take as long as it needs to, Mother. You won. I get to be fucking miserable for the rest of my life. But this, I'm taking for myself, and I don't care if it takes until next week." Bianca slammed the car door, shaking at the fury inside her that was mixed with a hefty dose of fear and anguish.

Would he even listen to what she had to say?

On unsteady legs, she headed inside the stables, fighting

back tears, not wanting to believe that this would be the last time she saw him.

She found him in the tack room. "Maverick."

His head whipped around at her voice. His eyes narrowed, and he glared. "I thought you were leaving to return to your fiancé in London."

"Can we talk, please? I need to explain," she pleaded.

He shook his head, dismissing her. "I don't have anything to say to you. You lied, princess. And not just a little white lie, but a big fucking one."

"I thought we... I just want to say that I'm sorry. I was going to tell you. I just hadn't decided—"

"Whether I was worth the headache, since I was just the guy you were fucking and having a little fun with, before you settled down to marry a duke, is that it?" he snapped furiously.

"No. That's not it at all." Tears streaked down her face. Why wouldn't he listen and give her a chance to explain?

"Well, as the guy you were just fucking... it's been fun. But we're done here," he said with such finality, her heart dropped through the floor.

Placing her hand on his forearm, she begged him. "If you would just listen—"

He yanked his arm away, his eyes blazing with wrath. "No, princess, you listen. I don't want you here. I don't want to see you ever again. Leave, run back to your fiancé, because I'm done with you. Being with you was the worst mistake of my life."

His words punched a hole clear through her chest, and left her gasping at the agony.

Maverick marched out of the tack room without glancing back, driving the final nail into the coffin of what they might have been. She clapped a hand over her mouth to contain her sob. Unsteady, fearing at any moment she was going to fall apart completely, she raced out of the tack room, past startled onlookers, including Tanner.

She climbed into the limo, ignoring her mother completely as her heart shattered into a million pieces. The car pulled away from the curb. As they drove past the green fields and rolling land of Silver Springs, a gulf of despair consumed Bianca.

Realization struck. She hadn't even got the chance to tell Sunshine goodbye. As the limo exited ranch property, she lowered her face into her hands, and wept.

24

Three days had passed since she had left.

Maverick worked the stables like a man possessed, unable to stop for fear of what he would have to face when he did. And he couldn't seem to move past the fact that she had slept with him when she was in love with and engaged to another man.

None of her actions made any sense. Not when he thought about all the intimacies they had shared. The way she had come alive for him.

Christ, he had no fucking clue what to do or how to feel.

He'd thought about calling her, not even sure whether the number he had would work any longer, or if she would answer a call from him. Because he needed to understand what the hell had happened, and why. He should have made her explain that day, before she left his life forever. But he'd been so fucking furious. And more hurt than he could ever remember being.

She'd agreed the night before to live with him. He believed they were moving toward a future together.

Sharing his living space was something he had never

offered another woman. Something he had never wanted with another woman until Bianca. And, for the first time in his life, he'd done the unthinkable.

He'd fallen for her.

Deeply.

Irrevocably.

He loved her with every breath in his body.

Deep in his gut, he knew he would *always* love her. And he very much feared she had ruined him for other women. That she was it for him.

He knocked on Amber's office door in response to the summons he had received. The same door that used to read *Colt Anderson, General Manager,* now read *Amber Anderson* with the same title.

"Come in," her voice carried through the door.

He pushed his way in but drew up short. Bianca's paintings were littered over every square inch of free surface available. He couldn't move as the agony slashed through him. Wasn't it already bad enough that he couldn't go visit his land without seeing her there?

Amber stood in the center of her office and nodded, with a frown marring her brow. "I know it's a lot. She had to leave them all behind, and told me I could do what I wanted with them. Sell them, donate them, put them in the trash."

He sucked in a shallow breath. "You talked to her? When?"

"Yesterday. She made it home. If you were wondering." Amber dangled the carrot.

He had been. And it was so strange, knowing how far away from him she was now. It was not like he would turn a corner in Winter Park, and she would be there. He could literally live out the rest of his days and never see her again. The thought of it made all the air leave his lungs.

Frustrated, angry, he snapped, "Why did you want to see me, Amber? I have a lot of work to get done today."

"Well, I wanted to ask you if there were any of the paintings that you wanted to keep before I made any decisions about them." She leveled him with a look, so like her brother's, but didn't blast him for the way he'd spoken to her.

He stared at the vibrant colors on the canvases. Memories assailed him.

"I don't want any of them," he protested. They would be a constant reminder of how worthless she considered him to be. How he'd been a way for her to pass the time, and nothing more. For someone like Mav, who had grown up having it drummed into him that he was a worthless mouth to feed and nothing more, that cut like thousands of knives. If he brought one of those portraits home, it would remind him every day just how worthless she had deemed him. He just couldn't do it.

"I understand. They're all excellent pieces. But there's one in particular, I think is meant for you." Amber pulled it out from a stack behind her.

Maverick sucked in a ragged breath the moment his eyes landed on it. Drawn to the image Bianca had created, he approached the painting. His heart beat rapidly in his chest. Bianca had a way of infusing a painting with rich, stunning life. But it was what was on this one that left him speechless, and almost took his legs out from under him.

It was *his* land. She had painted his property.

But not as it was now, just undeveloped forest, but what it could be once he crafted his home. She had taken the ideas and plans he had discussed with her, and brought them to life. In the middle, surrounded by the trees and mountains, was his house. She had included a barn and stables off to the side. There was even a small horse paddock.

Scanning the portrait, he found himself atop Black Jack, on the road, returning from their day at the ranch. But as he studied the house even closer, his gut clenched.

She had added to the house. On the opposite side of it, away from the barn and stable, there was an art studio, with a huge bank of windows to let the light stream inside. And standing at the front doorway, with a welcoming smile on her face, was Bianca. She had inserted herself into the vision of his home. The expression on her face was thrilled he was on his way home to her.

The painting was incredible in its detail, and utterly heartbreaking.

Oh, fuck!

"Why would she paint something like this?" he asked, his voice thick with emotion.

Amber sighed. "I won't divulge everything she told me. But I think she did it because she loves you."

"But she's engaged?" He shook his head, denying Amber's words. He couldn't start to think there was a possibility Bianca loved him. Because then, he would lose it.

"Which means, if you want to go stop her from marrying that guy, you're going to need to tell her how you feel," Amber explained with a somber expression.

"What, am I supposed to fly to London and tell her I love her, that she should marry me instead?"

Amber smiled. "I'm not telling you what you should do. Only that you have the paid vacation time available, if you decided to do something reckless like that."

Fly to London, and stop her from marrying that man. Tell her what she meant to him. That he was going out of his mind without her. Could he do it? Should he take that chance? Because the thought of flying there only to have her tell him no thanks, left him cold.

"I need to think about this," he replied.

"Well, think fast. The wedding is a week from Saturday. And if you need help getting a plane ticket, I'd be happy to give you your yearly bonus six months early."

Stunned at the generous offer, he asked, "Really? Why?"

"Because I think you two fit. And I can tell you the woman I talked to yesterday didn't sound like a woman excited about the prospect of her upcoming marriage. If anything, she sounded like a woman bound for the gallows."

"I need twenty-four hours. I'll give you my answer then." Was it possible Bianca truly didn't love the groom?

"Let me know. I'll be here," Amber said.

He strode to the door.

"Oh and Maverick, my money's on you. If I were placing bets on the outcome..." Amber said with a small shrug.

Hope filled him. Everyone who was anyone around here knew that Amber never bet with money. She didn't do poker or gambling of any kind. If she made a bet, it was because it was a sure thing. "Thanks. Your brother would be real proud of how you're managing this place."

"I appreciate that." Amber nodded.

Maverick left her office. His mind whirled at the possibilities and potential pitfalls of different courses of action. He tried to remember everything Bianca had explained about her family. What he remembered most, was how miserable discussing them had made her.

And from his brief interaction with her mother, he knew that woman had the personality of a rotten turnip. The only thing she had in common with her daughter was her looks. Because Bianca was the direct opposite of her mother. She was fierce and kind. And the stiff outer shell she had worn at their initial meeting, had begun to disintegrate.

Now that he had met Bianca's mom, that hard shell made much more sense.

He'd wanted to throttle the woman after two minutes. Maverick wondered at the strength in Bianca, having dealt with her mother her entire life, and was awed by it. Anyone else would have used it as an excuse to grow bitter and be just as vapid. But not his Bianca.

He was a fucking idiot for not hearing her out, for not fighting for her, and for them. She was the best damn thing that had ever happened to him, and the moment things got hard, he'd bailed. It hurt to breathe without her.

He didn't intend to live his life without her. Now, he simply had to figure out how to win his woman back.

25

*I*t had been four days since Bianca had been ripped from the love of her life.

And all her mother could do, as the dressmaker did the final fitting for the wedding dress, was pretend nothing had happened. Like Bianca's entire world hadn't crumbled into dust.

"You look lovely. Stop scowling or you're going to get wrinkles in your forehead and will then need to go see Doctor Burgess. Although, you are old enough to start getting some maintenance done. You'd only need to start with a few Botox injections on the forehead, make sure everything stays firm and youthful."

And on and on it went, ever since they had returned to London. Hell, ever since her mother had showed up on her doorstep, Bianca had felt like a ticking time bomb ready to explode. The dressmaker attached the veil to complete the fitting.

Bianca stared at her image in the mirror, feeling like she was wearing chains instead of a gorgeous wedding gown. Her mother stepped up onto the small raised fitting dais beside her. "There. Now you look good enough to marry a duke's son. A few weeks in the wilderness apparently did your body a world of good."

"Don't speak of it," Bianca warned through gritted teeth, and slanted a menacing glare at her.

But her mother always liked to go in for the kill, and couldn't help herself. "Oh, you mean you don't want me to tell your fiancé about the state I found you in?"

The threat hung heavy in the air. Bianca could see it all now. Any time she refused her mum, any time she tried to have something for herself, her mother would hold her being with Maverick over her head as leverage. And with it, not only would her heart continue to be ripped to shreds, she would slowly go mad.

A blinding, white hot fury bubbled up within her and blasted out. "That's it." Bianca ripped off the veil and tossed it to the floor. "I have had it up to here with you, Mother. I'm done. The wedding is off."

Her mum narrowed her eyes and stated in a frosty voice, "Don't you take that tone with me, young lady. Or are you forgetting what you stand to lose?"

That's all it ever was to her mother, all Bianca had ever been: a business transaction. The money, the estate and holdings—but absolutely no warm regard, or even simple kindness toward a fellow human being. Bianca snapped, "I've forgotten nothing you've done. And frankly, I don't give a blue fuck what happens to the estate. Give it to the Pope. Donate it to the ministry. I don't care. I'm not going to marry a man I don't love, or live anywhere near you." She gripped the material of the sleeve and yanked as hard as she could. It was better than doing what she really wanted to do —which was clock her mum with a good right hook.

The dressmaker gasped as the gown ripped down the

side. But Bianca reveled in the sound and sight of it. She was in a full-blown fury, and enjoying the ride for a change. Her wrath was decades in the making.

Her mother narrowed her eyes even further, into angry slits. "If you do this, you will be completely cut off."

Bianca's laughter sounded crazy, even to her ears, but she no longer gave two shits what her mum or anyone else thought. "Then I'll be cut off. At least I won't have to look at your stupid face or listen to your idle prattle any more. If I have to attend one more ridiculous ladies' tea with you and your friends, I will start gouging eyes out with the teaspoons —starting with you. And I really don't care that you don't want to be in my life, because frankly, I don't want you in mine."

"You're ruining everything your father and I have built."

For the first time in her life, Bianca saw fear in her mother's eyes. "Maybe you should have asked me even once what *I* wanted for my life, instead of trying to control me and make me live yours."

Her mum reared back at the controlled fury in her voice. As Bianca glared, she realized this would be the last time she would see her mother. And she was all right with that. Her mother had made her choices. It was time Bianca made hers. She left the dais, and headed to the changing room to remove the tattered gown, not wasting any time removing the bloody thing and donning her clothes.

"You're not seriously going back to that man, are you?" her mum sneered outside the changing room.

"If he'll have me. Yes." Bianca drew the curtain back.

"This is so typical of you. It's why I had to pay that Rafael guy off all those years ago." Her mother shook her head.

Wait, what? Bianca shot her mother a glare as she

grabbed her handbag. "You mean Renaud? You paid Renaud to what, stop seeing me?"

Her heart beat fast as she thought about the sudden change in Renaud all those years past.

"Of course! I couldn't allow my daughter to commit herself to a man like that. It doesn't matter that he wanted to marry you—"

Pain slashed through Bianca. Renaud had been another Moonbeam. Her mother had orchestrated the breakup, sure that once Bianca was devastated about the ending, she would be more malleable to control, and convince to return to London. She snarled, "Leave. Right now. While you still have a chance. I don't ever want to see you again."

"Always so dramatic." Her mum rolled her eyes.

With her hands shaking, Bianca said, "Well, if you're not leaving, I am. Goodbye, Mother."

"You walk out of that door, don't ever contact your father or me again," were her mum's parting words as Bianca slammed the door behind her on her way out.

She should be sad, but all she felt toward her mum was fury. Her mother had paid Renaud to claim he didn't love her. It had devastated Bianca.

And she had almost let her do it once more with Maverick. Out of fear, she had allowed her mum to interject herself into the relationship, and land the barbed words certain to cause the most heartbreak.

Bianca was done with her. And she was finished with London too. She didn't want to be here. She wanted to be where the land reached up and touched the clouds. She wanted Maverick to give her another chance.

Oh, fuck!

She was moving to America. There were so many things

she needed to do to make that happen. Her heart pounded as she walked.

But there was one thing left for her to do before she could start on her plans for her future. She checked the time.

It was time she broke the news to Peter. It was better if it came from her, and not her mother or the gossipmongers.

He should be home at this hour. She took a cab across town, making calls along the way to her banker, to have him start setting up accounts and working with a bank in the United States. She had to hire movers. The furniture in her flat could be sold at auction. She had a friend, Molly, who ran one of the auction houses, and made a mental note to call her. The easiest thing to do would be to just buy new furniture over there instead of paying ghastly shipping fees. Honestly, all those things were a reminder of her life in London. And she didn't want any of it.

It wasn't until she arrived at Peter's doorstep that Bianca grew nervous. But she wouldn't let fear stop her. After paying the cab driver, she took the steps at a fast clip. She was relieved that she didn't have to wait long for him to answer the door.

Peter was a dashing man, with chocolate brown eyes and a full head of blond hair. He was kind and smart, and everything she should want. But she knew, standing here looking at him, that she was making the right decision.

"Here's my bride to be, this is a surprise," Peter said, ushering her inside.

"Peter, we need to talk," Bianca said as he escorted her into the living room full of big, comfortable leather sofas.

"Oh, sounds serious. What's this about, Bee?" he said, using the nickname from her childhood.

"I'm sorry, but I can't marry you," she blurted out before she lost her nerve.

Peter's eyes widened and then he sank down onto a chair. "Oh, thank god."

"What? You don't want to marry me either?" She almost laughed at the situation, and took a seat beside him.

He gripped one of her hands and stared at her. "Bee, you know I love you like a sister. But no, we've both been bound by the arrangement our parents established fifteen years ago. You're sure about this?"

"Yes, one hundred percent. I just had it out with my mum at the dressmaker's. Told her I was calling it off."

Peter grimaced. "How'd she take it?"

"How do you think?" Bianca asked drolly, given he knew her mother well.

"That bad, eh? Well, I'm so relieved. Now we will be free to..." Peter appeared unsettled and shifted in his seat, dropping his gaze from her.

"Has there been someone else?" she asked, feeling more lighthearted by the second.

"Yes. She's working class. My parents will be up in arms over it, but I love Anna," Peter said with a look in his eyes Bianca knew well. It was the same one that crossed her face when she thought of Maverick.

She gave him a big hug. "I'm so happy for you, and frankly, relieved. I hate that I put you through all this and couldn't end it sooner. We should have. And you should know, while I was away in the United States, I met someone. And, well..." She trailed off.

Peter cast her a lopsided grin. "The heart wants what it wants. So, an American, eh? Guess I won't be seeing you at the club or around London, will I?"

Tears threatened. Out of all the people in London, he

was going to be one of the few whom she would genuinely miss. "No. I may come back to visit. My mother said I'll be cut off, and I honestly no longer care what the woman does. But my god, do you know what it's like to not have to worry that you're going to offend someone who could shame your family for generations?"

"Absolutely not. It sounds bloody amazing. Your mum will forgive you eventually."

Bianca shook her head. "No. I don't think she will. She doesn't have it in her, and I no longer care to try."

"When do you leave?"

"In a few days. As soon as I can get my affairs sorted."

"But you'll stay in touch, Bee, please? We've been friends almost our entire lives. And I for one will miss your commentary at our functions," Peter said, rising from his seat.

"I will." She hugged him. "Now, go and call Anna and tell her you're a free man. I wish you both nothing but happiness."

After another hug goodbye at the door, Bianca left Peter's house for her flat. She had every intention to be boarding a plane for America in seventy-two hours or less if she could manage it. And then she would throw her heart at Maverick's feet, and pray that he would forgive her.

26

It took Bianca a few days to put her affairs in order and arrange for a visa to stay in the United States. She was lucky that she had a friend in the State Department who knew a guy, and now she was the proud owner of a work visa—so that she could paint the American West.

Her dad, while disappointed, understood her decision, and was taking care of cancelling the ceremony and getting the gifts sent back to the senders. He promised to work on her mother. Bianca doubted it would do any good. But he did promise that he wouldn't allow her mum to cut her out of the will.

Frankly, if she did, she did. Bianca had inherited an estate from both sets of grandparents, and was quite wealthy in her own right.

But there were the banking issues and such she had to see to if she was planning on making her move to the States permanent. And even if Maverick no longer wanted her, she doubted she would ever want to go back to England to live. To go back for a visit? Not for a very long time. Perhaps for Peter and Anna's wedding next year. She was thrilled that he was so happy.

But now she sat in a rental SUV, parked right outside the Silver Springs Ranch stables, with her heart clogging her throat. She had let Amber know that she was returning, and planned on staying this time. Amber had offered her a room at her house if Maverick turned her down.

Her heart trembled. If he didn't want her... then she would make her decisions from there. But until she knew whether there was a chance for them or not, she was going with the belief that he did care for her.

His truck was parked out front, so she knew he was around. Before she chickened out, she forced herself to climb out of the vehicle and went searching for the man.

She walked through the stables, and almost burst into tears when Sunshine poked her head over her stall in greeting.

"Hey, sweetheart." Bianca approached the mare and patted her nose. "I've missed seeing you."

Sunshine nudged her shoulder. "Not today. But maybe tomorrow we could go for a ride, just you and me."

"Bianca, what are you doing here?"

She turned and found Tanner glaring at her with a deep, furrowed scowl. She deserved it. She had hurt one of his best friends due to the secret she had kept. Her voice thick, she asked, "Where is he?"

"Meeting some real estate guy back at his place." Tanner shrugged.

"What?" she gasped.

"He's selling his property. Not really sure why." Tanner's stare was full of accusation. It told Bianca that *she* was the reason Maverick was selling the land he loved.

"What do you mean, he's selling his property?" She gripped Tanner's forearm.

"It's what he told me he was doing this afternoon. Meeting with a real estate agent about putting it on the market. Why does it matter to you?" Tanner asked.

"He can't sell it. He loves that place. I need to go there, now. Stop him."

He shrugged her hand off. "That's up to him."

"Please, help me stop him. Can I take Sunshine? I'll pay for the ride. I don't need a guide." She knew the way by heart.

He cocked his head. "Depends. Are you still engaged to the duke? Or are you staying this time?"

"No. I called it off. If he'll have me, then yes, I'm staying."

The corners of Tanner's mouth curled up. "Come with me, and we can get her saddled right quick."

"Thank you, Tanner."

It felt like it took forever to get Sunshine saddled, but likely was only minutes. With her heart pounding in her chest, Bianca took off. Today she didn't pay attention to the beauty of the mountains or the stream she and Sunshine followed. Her sole focus was reaching Maverick in time.

They raced over the trail. Sunshine's hooves pounded against the ground as Bianca gave her her head and let her race. They covered a great distance quickly. They crested the last small ridge that opened up onto the meadowed vista of his land, and she spied Maverick shaking hands with a guy in a gray suit before the gentleman climbed into his truck.

"Wait!" she yelled, kicking her heels into Sunshine's flanks and spurring her onward.

Maverick turned her way as the truck rolled on past, his

gaze unreadable and his face impassive. She drank him in as she and Sunshine galloped directly toward him. He was so bloody handsome in his jeans and hat. And while it had only been a week since she had seen him, it felt like a life-time had passed since she had touched him, felt the immutable strength of his arms around her.

When she reached his side, Bianca dismounted from Sunshine, dropping her reins to let her graze.

His face shuttered, Mav asked, "Why are you here? Won't your fiancé be worried?"

"I'm not marrying Peter. I ended the engagement. I couldn't marry him. And you can't sell this place. Maverick, you love this land. Why would you sell it?"

"Why can't you marry Peter?" he barreled right over her question.

The two of them could do the biting back and forth all day. It was time she came clean and cleared the air. Then they would see.

"I need you to know a few things. I never meant to hide the engagement from you. I just wasn't sure what to do about it. I didn't say anything that first night because I figured that would be it between us. You need to under-stand, our parents betrothed us as teenagers, because they're still stuck a few hundred years in the past, where society and prestige matter. And I can't marry him because we've never been more than friends. I'm not, nor have I ever been, in love with him, nor he with me. We've never even slept together. Peter thanked me for calling it off. He didn't want to marry me either but was bound by the same conventions I had been—until I decided I wanted something different. My parents have cut me off. I sincerely doubt my mother will ever speak to me again after I called off the wedding.

And if you're truly set on selling your land, then I will buy it."

"Why are you here, princess?" he asked, unmoving and wary.

A gasket inside her blew. She gestured wildly in her frustration. "Isn't it obvious? If it's not, then I will spell it out for you. Because I am truly, madly, deeply in love with you. And I was hoping that you could find it in your heart to forgive me for keeping the engagement a secret from you. I didn't expect to fall for you. When I suggested we should sleep together that first time, I figured it would be a fun diversion. But the moment you touched me, I was yours. Is there even a chance you might consider dating me again?"

"No." He shook his head.

With a single word from him, her heart crashed and burned. Everything inside her seized up at the stark agony infiltrating the furthest reaches of her soul. He didn't want her. "I see. Then I will... leave, and promise not to bother you again."

Bianca turned, her eyes blinded with tears. She had been so certain he had feelings for her. She reached for Sunshine's reins. A rough hand shot out, grabbed her by the shoulders, and spun her around.

Lips crashed down over hers, a torrent of need exploded, and she clutched at him. Her tears fell as she kissed him back. She whimpered under his greedy assault. Her body liquified at feeling his arms around her, holding her tight.

Maverick tore his mouth from hers but didn't release her. His eyes were pure spun gold, and were filled with so much emotion, she trembled. "You didn't let me finish. I don't want to date you anymore because I want to marry you. I love you, princess. You're it for me, too. And I was selling my place so I could head to London and be where you are, because I don't want to live without you. Even if all I would have been able to do was watch you from afar."

"You were going to move to London? For me?" In all her life, no one had ever even considered making such a sacrifice for her, let alone actually taken steps toward doing it.

"Yep. So, you going to marry me or what, princess?" He quirked a brow, a hint of a smile curling at the corners of his lips.

Did she want to marry him? "There's nothing I want more."

"Is that right?" The grin spread across his face, the one she loved more than anything.

"But what about this place? Is it too late for you to get it back?" she asked, afraid he had taken irreversible steps that he would come to regret.

"I haven't sold it yet. I've had some offers, but it seems I might have waited just long enough for the best one yet. I'm sorry your parents cut you off. I don't want you to worry about money. I make more than enough to support both of us."

"Maverick." She sighed and kissed him, her heart bursting with more joy than it could possibly contain. But before they passed the point of no return, she removed her mouth and said, "That's not going to be an issue at all—the money, I mean."

His big hands caressed up and down her back. "I know it's not. We'll make it work until you sell your paintings, or do whatever it is you want to do."

The poor man was in for another shock. This was one of those things she hadn't mentioned either. "No, what I meant was even though my parents cut me off, they could only do it with their estate. I'm an only grandchild, with two sets of extremely well-off grandparents who doted on me and left their estates to me—and neither of my parents have ever had access to those funds or accounts. Money is never going to be an issue for us. In fact, in full disclosure, you're not just marrying a Brit, but an extremely wealthy one. And I was thinking about that house you wanted to build here... would you be averse to a few additions?"

He cupped her face in his hands, his eyes blazing with love. "As long as I have you, I have everything I could possibly want or need. Whatever you want for our home, if you don't want to live here and need to live in a big city, or—"

She placed her hand over his mouth to stop him. "I would never take you away from a place you love."

He gripped her wrist and removed her fingers from his mouth. "But I love you more. You are the most important part of my life. I can find land anywhere, but there's only one of you."

Maverick stepped back and knelt in the grass on one knee.

"I figure we should do this all formal like." He gripped her hand in his and drew a small black box from his back pocket.

"Bianca, I never figured I would fall in love, or ever want to tie myself to one woman. But what I didn't realize was all I was doing was biding my time until you arrived. You challenge me, make me a better man, and Dom. I never knew I could love someone this much. I want you as my wife and partner. I want babies with you. I want to build our home and our life together. You're it for me, princess. Marry me."

"Yes, a thousand times, yes." Joy spilled from her heart

and radiated out. She couldn't stop the happy tears from escaping when he slid the ring over her finger.

Maverick rose and drew her in, his eyes shining with love for her. And she had no regrets about leaving her old life behind. When he kissed her, her heart expanded, every part of her being in tune with him.

"You're not worried that I'm not the greatest cook?" she asked him in between kisses.

He shook his head. "Nah. I'll never be entirely house-broken, so we're even on that end. Besides, just how loaded are we talking? Enough to hire someone to cook for us?"

She chuckled. "That's a very real possibility. And I don't mind at all, you see, because I have a big thing for my rough cowboy. There's no one who loves me like he does. In fact, I was hoping he didn't have to head back to work just yet, and would love me right now."

"Always, and then I'm taking you home, where I'm not letting you out of my bed for the rest of the night."

Anticipation fluttered in her belly. "I like the sound of that, Sir."

Bianca sighed as he took her mouth, lifted her up into his arms, and carried her to the secluded spot beneath the pines. It was their spot. One she knew, as he lowered her gently to the ground, they would visit often.

It was the place where she had fallen for him. It was the place where they would build their home, raise children together, and spend their forever.

And she couldn't wait to start living it.

The End

HOW TO ROPE A LOYAL COWBOY
SILVER SPRINGS RANCH SERIES, BOOK 4

Widowed single dad Noah needs help in the worst way. He's desperate to find a new live-in nanny to care for his four-year-old twins while he's at work in the stables. Ever since his wife died, he has lived like a monk. What with raising two boys solo and working as the horse master for Silver Springs Ranch, there hasn't been time in his life for things like finding a willing bed partner to slake his dark needs.

When the achingly beautiful Morgan appears on his doorstep inquiring about the job, he doesn't think twice about hiring her. He snaps her up before she discovers his boys are little hellions who have driven the last few nannies away over their antics.

And yet, for the first time in three years, since he buried his heart in the ground, Noah is entranced by naughty visions of the new nanny. She's young, full of enthusiasm, and stirs up every wicked fantasy in his arsenal.

He prays he has the fortitude to resist her delectable charms because she's forbidden. At his age, he can't sleep with, let alone crave, a woman fresh out of college. But she keeps casting sexy glances suffused with desire in his direction, battering his resolve to stay away. She's headstrong, and he aches to exert his dominance.

Will he wave the white flag, and surrender to her naughty whispered pleas?

Get it now!

MIDNIGHT MASQUERADE
DUNGEON SINGLES NIGHT SERIES, BOOK 1

Sophia is in trouble. Again.

Maybe it's the masks. Maybe she needs to feel something other than regret.

Whatever the reason, she is either daring... or foolish... when she trades places with another submissive, and ends up spending the night in her mysterious boss's bed.

He doesn't recognize her, but now she's had him, she knows one taste of his dark love will never be enough.

Gabriel Ryan has one firm rule: don't sleep with employees.

Even though he's infuriated beyond measure to discover Sophia in his bed after a night of mind-blowing pleasure, she is now in his blood. He craves her. Needs her. Yearns for her surrender.

But she is forbidden. He will break her with his dark desires.

When Sophia's dangerous past waltzes into his club, Gabriel must protect her. He must claim her. And break every single one of his rules to keep her safe.

Head to Eternal Eros! Get it now!

ALSO BY ANYA SUMMERS

Dungeon Singles Night Series

Midnight Masquerade

Midnight Mystique

Midsummer Night's Dream

Silver Springs Ranch Books

How To Rope A Wild Cowboy

How To Rope A Rich Cowboy

How To Rope A Rough Cowboy

How To Rope A Loyal Cowboy

The Manor Series

The Man In The Mask

Torn In Two

Redeemed By Love

The Man In The Mask: The Complete Manor Series Collection

ABOUT ANYA

Born in St. Louis, Missouri, Anya grew up listening to Cardinals baseball and reading anything she could get her hands on. She remembers her mother saying if only she would read the right type of books instead binging her way through the romance aisles at the bookstore, she'd have been a doctor. While Anya never did get that doctorate, she graduated cum laude from the University of Missouri-St. Louis with an M.A. in History.

Anya is a bestselling and award-winning author published in multiple fiction genres. She also writes urban fantasy, paranormal romance, and contemporary romance under the name Maggie Mae Gallagher. A total geek at her core, when she is not writing, she adores attending the latest comic con or spending time with her family. She currently lives in the Midwest with her two furry felines.

www.anyasummers.com
anya@anyasummers.com

Join Anya's mailing list to be the first to be notified of new releases, free books, exclusive content, special prizes and author giveaways!
https://anyasummers.com/newsletter/

Follow Anya on social media!

Facebook: facebook.com/AnyaSummersAuthor

Twitter: twitter.com/anyabsummers

Instagram: instagram.com/anyasummersauthor

Goodreads: goodreads.com/author/show/
15183606.Anya_Summers

BookBub: bookbub.com/authors/anya-summers